Praise for This World D

"A deliciously menacing read which I just couldn't put down. Every word punches hard. *This World Does Not Belong to Us* treads the fine line between beauty and horror effortlessly."
JAN CARSON, author of *The Raptures*

"Visceral prose. ... There is a strange, unconventional beauty to Lucas's morbid world—a beauty that helps him endure pain and humiliation and achieve an unnerving final calm. *This World Does Not Belong to Us* is a bleak exploration of how all ends in death and decay."
Foreword Reviews

"One of the debut novels that most stood out this year in Latin America."
New York Times

"García Freire manages to make us sweat with her characters. Feel the sting of their bites. This novel demonstrates a salient maturity, exudes literary knowledge, and takes risks. The writer masters the world of emotions and the words to encapsulate it."
El País

"Who would have thought that a novel so overflowing with animals, insects, flowers, and shrubs could teach us so much about ourselves?"
Latin American Literature Today

"Tremendous, a delight."
MÓNICA OJEDA, author of *Mandíbula*

"This book is pure beauty, pure love for the written word."
COPE Blogs

"García Freire takes us to the deepest parts of the human condition."
Página Dos

"Full of courage and lucidity, Natalia García Freire writes against the current; she doesn't care about hype or dogmas. Her writing is inhabited by the voices of literary masters. What a mature novel from a twenty-nine-year-old who knows so much about life, the passing of time, old age, the absence of God and death. There are books that can only be written by those who love plants devastatingly. This is one of them."
El Universo

This
World
Does
Not
Belong
to
Us

NATALIA GARCÍA FREIRE

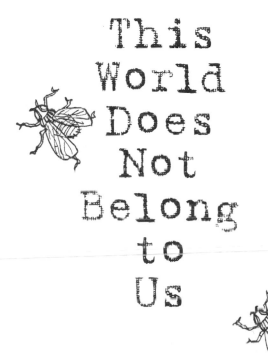

This World Does Not Belong to Us

Translated from the Spanish
by Victor Meadowcroft

WORLD EDITIONS
New York, London, Amsterdam

Published in the USA in 2022 by World Editions LLC, New York

World Editions
New York / London / Amsterdam

World Editions is committed to a sustainable future. Papers used by World
Editions meet the FSC standards of certification.

Printed by Lake Book, USA

Library of Congress Cataloging in Publication Data is available

ISBN 978-1-64286-115-0

First published as *Nuestra piel muerta* in Spain and Latin America in 2019 by
La Navaja Suiza
UK edition published in 2022 by Oneworld Publications, London

This book has been selected to receive financial assistance from English PEN's
PEN Translates programme, supported by Arts Council England. English PEN
exists to promote literature and our understanding of it, to uphold writers'
freedoms around the world, to campaign against the persecution and impris-
onment of writers for stating their views, and to promote the friendly cooper-
ation of writers and the free exchange of ideas. www.englishpen.org

Twitter: @WorldEdBooks
Facebook: @WorldEditionsInternationalPublishing
Instagram: @WorldEdBooks
YouTube: World Editions
www.worldeditions.org

Book Club Discussion Guides are available on our website.

For Matías and Bartleby (our cat)

"We listen to insects
and human voices
with different ears"

KOBAYASHI ISSA

Table of Contents

I don't believe my dead father is watching me. But his body is buried in this garden, what is left of my mother's garden, surrounded by slugs, camel spiders, earthworms, ants, beetles, and woodlice. Perhaps there's even some scorpion that sits beside my father's semi-decomposed face, together resembling the depictions in an Egyptian pharaoh's tomb.

We buried him near this spot where I'm resting, behind these stone statues. If I scrabbled all night, I might come across him. Who knows whether I would first grab hold of his hands or his feet or the ends of his black suit pants? Who knows how his body may have repositioned itself in order to rest in peace? We buried him without so much as changing that old suit he was wearing, because the body was starting to smell.

Everything happened so quickly that it's only now, after these many nights and days have passed, that I'm beginning to think of him as truly dead, dead enough to return and haunt a place. And at night I sometimes speak to him.

If you're watching me right now, father: I've come home. Although it seems more like I've come back to some other place, some other time, some other world, in which we never existed. I'm sorry if I occasionally get distracted and focus, incessantly, on the things you called worthless. But right now, surrounded by all those earthworms, you must be thinking these things weren't so unimportant after all, right? If they get in through your mouth and your ears and even, who knows, through your anus, and gnaw away at you through the night; if they traverse your body from top to bottom searching for anything left of you they can use, and then settle upon your hands and feet and wriggle. Don't you think that, after our deaths, after everything, it is they who are the stronger ones? And that, all things considered, perhaps this world does not belong to us, but to those miniscule beings, so numerous that they could bury us completely if they ever came together.

Cover the entire Earth, like a huge carpet that from outer space would look black and shiny.

This is not our home, father. It hasn't been for a long time. I think you already knew that, which is why you let yourself be killed. Isn't that true, father? Isn't that what happened? You let yourself be killed. And isn't it also true that no one could have helped you, because what you wanted was to go. Go once and for all. Even if by the shortest route.

Damn it, father. You always chose the shortest route.

I've come home, but have not yet dared go in. They're still there. I watched them dine on quails this evening, and as I stood before the door I shuddered.

Childishness, you say? Bah! What are you saying, father? In the time since you've been dead I've grown, and while working Señor Elmur's land—because, yes, that's where they took me, father, to till foreign soil—my arms became strong and brown, and my legs, scrawny as they were, are now capable of crushing the skull of a small animal, a monkey, or perhaps a cat, or let's say a rat, with a single blow. There's no childishness, father. But you can't see this because you're lying down there, dead. And you're the one to blame. And you know it. Remember, it was you who insisted that they stay a little longer? That we ought to look out for strangers and treat them as our brothers. That God commanded this, and God commanded that. Well, tell that God of yours they're now sleeping in your bed, wearing your clothes, and have left your body lying beneath the earth in your own garden, so they can trample over it each day.

Your body, father, which in its shrunken state must now resemble mine more than either of us can imagine.

This earth is like a mirror.

Me on one side. You on the other.

CEMETERY FLIES

No one calls me Lucas anymore, father.

Though I may have relinquished my name, I did once have a family. Our house waits for me like a succession of dreams in which I'm unable to stop falling. I arrived here drawn by it, by this house with its yellow walls and scabbed earth.

I traveled barefoot up and down hills, walking over naked earth, over rocks and plains, dead earth cobbled with tombstones. I left behind all those paths swept by wind and breeze and, the closer I came, the more I could sense this foul air that now envelops everything in this place, escaping through cracks in the old adobe walls, through the gaps left by the wallpaper that peels away like dead skin; this air that appears to obscure the space until it attains a sepia-like tone of abandonment, leaving behind deposits of all those indefinite forms of filth.

Crouching like some kind of vermin, I spy on the house. About my head swarm flies, minute and razor-sharp, cemetery flies. I envision them flying over imaginary countries. It's a miniature war. Below, the ants, marching single file across the tiled floor, are soldiers preparing for an attack on the last crumbling fortress. I rest my fingers on the wooden window frame and examine the hollows left by moths. Cannonballs!

High above these near-secret beings there's another world, full of great catastrophes.

Which does not matter.

You used to go on tirelessly about how I didn't focus on what was useful. "For the love of God, Lucas! That's not important," you would tell me every time I prepared to launch into some story about the insects inhabiting my mother's garden: caterpillars that advanced one after another, as in procession, devouring weeds; praying mantises that captured hummingbirds and elegantly ingested them; red ants that banded together to form rafts for the crossing of small puddles.

You were right, father. The dead always are.

It's true, I don't focus on what's useful. I notice insignificant things, waste my time on trifles. I believe the greater an event, the more easily it fades away. We Torrente de Valses disappeared from town, and it's like nothing ever happened. They happily wrote my mother off as mad, after all, they'd always yearned to be able to declare it openly: "We saw it coming, Josefina never came to mass and she wasn't baptized." This is what was said in the market lanes by respectable-looking ladies—which is to say, ladies who were horrid but well dressed.

And even the fact I'd been sold into slavery was seen as something good, something deserved, because what else could be done with the child of a madwoman?

There's nothing left of us, father, except for these tiny animals attracted by the warmth surrounding death. More alive than the living who walk and talk.

Squatting down, I peek inside the house, with only my head appearing in the window, like the Devil. "God sees all, Lucas," is what you always used to say. But I no longer believe this. God is far too prim and proper for that. The Devil, on the other hand, must be a real voyeur. And so am I.

I peer through the windowpane, the raindrops acting as magnifying glasses, but everything looks blurry. I have to strain to see. It looks as if it's all still there. The living room with the antique diamond-patterned armchairs where my mother used to sit and read, the Bentwood benches, the dining room at the back. Felisberto is sitting in your place, father, at the head of the table, with Eloy to his right. The evening light coming through the front window softens their features, as if they were but a pair of shepherds. They're having quails for dinner. Such a fondness for quails! For eating them whole. They grab them by the legs, leaving their bones picked clean from nape to talon. They're wearing your clothes, that pair of grey flannel jackets, and still sport those long, grisly beards, flecked with bits of beer foam.

Things inside the house haven't changed

since I left. The portraits of the grandfathers are still visible on the wall behind Felisberto, as are the burnt-out candles on the table, the Persian rug, the dusty china dinner set in the cabinet in the corner topped with glass bottles of sulphate, tartrate, and bicarbonate, bottles as white as bone and with the scent of an apothecary's shop; the bargueño chest on the adjacent table, with its secret drawers in which my mother kept desiccated flowers for her herbariums; even the tablecloth is the one we used on the last day we all sat down to eat together, the only tablecloth my mother ever knitted.

Everything is there, father, but nothing speaks of us.

Those two men in the paintings, the grandfathers, could be any old men, short and solemn-looking.

One would think that, having held us inside it for so long, the least this house could do would be to conspire to entrap the intruders, like a spider: spinning its web and keeping them in there until they dried out. But houses also grow old and forget.

From somewhere, Noah and Sarai appear.

They walk gazing blankly, in those starched smock uniforms Esther makes them wear, dressed up like dolls. They remove the plates of quail from the table and serve two baskets of fruit, bread, and toasted corn nuts. Eloy doesn't hesitate, snatching the food from the receptacles. I look at his face, that face devoid of a chin, the trembling jowls, the permanently flared nostrils; I watch him eat, become an idiot, scraps of food dropping everywhere, eyes always on the move. Anything he doesn't like he throws on the floor.

Perhaps this was the thing that most frightened us about Eloy, this semblance of a village idiot who might at any moment be capable of killing us all and then heading out to eat roasted broad beans on the patio, in the genteel shadow of the elm.

Felisberto, on the other hand, is cunning. Cunning as a guinea pig, as Esther used to say. Like a circus ringmaster, there's never any doubt about the limits of his wickedness and vulgarity. He implements these fearlessly. I know him well.

When Sarai removes his plate, his hand is already at her waist and climbs up to her breasts as, with the other hand, he snatches up another quail's wing by its delicate bone. I imagine him saying: "A man can't live on bread alone!" The kind of thing Felisberto used to say and that you, father, applauded. But I can't hear anything; I only see that he is laughing.

I crouch down and rest my back against the wall. A smell of urine, which may come from my clothes or from the gaps between the tiles, somehow relaxes me. This has always been the case; perhaps that's why I was so fond of the chamber pot that used to be left inside my room in case I needed to pee. Sometimes I would wake in the middle of the night, lie there rigid as a tree trunk, and experience a primitive form of fear: the fear of fear. Then I'd make for the chamber pot, the room filling for a moment with vapor, and be sent back to sleep by that pleasant rustlike smell that comes from each of us.

Now the sun sets in the distance and the hills are changing color, becoming their own shadows; the paths darken and stray and the trees nearby do not move, because here, in this house, there's no longer any wind and everything is still.

What have I come in search of, father? Silence? An illusion? A homeland?

The one who returns is nameless, knows not what he seeks, and lives as a guest in his own home.

Perhaps I should have stayed away, as my mother told me to: "Say you'll leave here forever, Lucas! Swear it!" This is what she said to me one day at the Sisters of Saint Mariana Sanatorium. A place where everything expires, the end of ending. It was hard to find, but I saw it, father. There aren't even any gardens; only good and evil, heaven and hell: rooms for the nuns and rooms for the sufferers. "Swear it, Lucas!" my mother begged me, gripping my hand urgently, because the nuns with hairs protruding from their moles were taking her away. And I looked directly into her eyes, which were already fading. I looked back at her mutely, as though from inside a mirror.

And I didn't heed her advice.

I didn't heed her advice because, as they carried me away from this house, something emerging as though from my sternum became taut and pulled me back, as if I'd been born chained to this land. Just as the winds are chained to the mountains.

And perhaps it's for the best that you sent my mother away, father, because if she could see her garden now, she might die from sheer sorrow, as I always imagined she would. There's nothing left but the stone animals she had carved, scattered like remnants of an extinct civilization, covered in vines and mildew, and the roots of the solitary elm have surfaced, full of moss, its branches desiccated.

All of the rosebushes are dead. The chrysanthemums too.

Of the wallflowers, there remain only small stalks with projecting slivers, like mutilated tree trunks. The spiral of buds that used to overflow with different colors now contains nothing but a few clusters of Chinese bellflowers and some cockscombs. The rest of the garden has been invaded by brambles, poppies, crabgrass, and thistles that prickle me where my pants are torn.

I pull up dandelions and chew them root

first, resting my head on the ground of the invaded garden. The memory of my mother rings out among the dead plants. Or perhaps it's the cicadas, singing for my return.

THE NIGHT THE COWS LOWED

That long day was growing cold and the cows would not cease their lowing. Esther had set about braiding the hair of my nursemaids, pulling the strands tightly as if strangling miniscule beings between the black hairs.

"The master will have to put them down," she muttered under her breath. "And they won't even yield good meat," she added.

No one responded, and she carried on tugging at the disordered strands on that cold, dirty night. Every evening that month had seemed filled with dust, while the days brimmed with a milky light and little dry flowers that floated on the ponds. Time had become faltering, impeded by that sound, a purulent sound, draining. Anyone walking over by the cows was assaulted by nausea, for the lowing emanated as if from an ulcerated stomach and a parched larynx.

To begin with we assumed the cows were in heat. First we took them over to the bulls belonging to the Moratti brothers, but the cows refused to breed, spurning them like the plague; then Esther, Noah, and I dragged them to where Father Hetz's bulls were grazing; after that we made them cross the entire town to reach the farm of Señor Manzi, the owner of the town's most sought-after stud.

I remember how, when we reached Señor Manzi's farm, the sun was hiding and the air was dense, the sky neither yellow nor grey but a troubling mixture of the two. Ten meters from that stud, who Señor Manzi had baptized Brazen, the cows turned to stone, immobile, huddled together, as though an invisible wall had been planted before their faces. They stretched their necks and let their tails fall still. They looked at Brazen for a few minutes and we felt this was the day they would finally cease their lowing, but nothing happened. At first Esther feigned patience, but soon her breathing grew heavy as she tugged at the halters to bring the cows closer, chivvying them angrily and occasionally sniffling, because the strong wind had given her a runny nose. Señor Manzi assisted her, baiting them and whistling at them, but the cows just threw themselves down in the grass and continued their disconsolate lowing. That day, Esther swore she would never again take those blessed cows anywhere.

However, that wasn't the reason they were lowing. We didn't know it yet, but we had already surrendered.

Noah, Mara, and Sarai allowed their hair to be braided on that cold, dirty night, sitting side-on inside the large room where they slept in four old narrow beds with tall steel frames, like those of boarding schools, hospices, and sanatoriums. When my nursemaids had their hair braided, they resembled different women; their plump bodies escaped from the starched smock uniforms, their woven sashes were unwound and the blouses came loose, dropped off, and crumpled. Sarai's white brassiere became visible, embroidered very close to the nipple.

That night, I tried to recall what her nipples looked like. It had been Sarai who'd given me her breast when I was born because mamá's milk dried up. Her small breasts were barely noticeable back then, like the mounds of dirt where I collected earthworms. But hard as I tried, I could not remember how her nipples looked. Sometimes I spent hours trying, with eyes squeezed shut, but all that appeared were breasts painted with doll's nipples, ugly nipples, nothing more. Memory, when unable to recall, distorts. You, father, I sometimes remember like Napoleon before he was exiled, that Napoleon at Fontainebleau from the history books Professor Erlano used to bring when he gave me lessons, a Napoleon with an expanding waistline and thinning hair, and, above all, a defeated demeanor. And the truth is that you were dark and skinny and had all that slicked-back hair on top of your head, but hard as I try, I'm unable to combine these notions into something resembling a father.

The lowing that night was worse, seeming to push up against the walls of the house, pass through them, and echo in the corners. It was an intrusive sound, desperate. I wandered around the house, searching for slugs by following the shiny, viscous trail they left on the floor and walls, wanting to gather them up and take them to the garden before Esther could throw salt on them. But there weren't even any slugs; perhaps the sound had driven them all into hiding.

I made for the diamond-patterned sofa in the living room, where mamá was looking out of the window with an open book in her lap. I knew this wasn't her looking out at the world, but something out there looking in at her. She had that stillness of someone who knows they're being observed, like a bird watched through binoculars or an insect studied under a magnifying glass. Her skin was so fine, it sometimes seemed as though all her veins would surface like the roots of an invisible tree that has started to walk, crossing her heart and chest and liberating her from herself. I rested my head on the petticoat covering her legs. It smelled of flowers and mothballs. Mamá didn't detect my presence, continuing to stare out of the window.

You, father, emerged from your study, leaving a trail of pipe smoke in your wake, and told us to go up to our rooms. My mother, not shifting her gaze from the window, said only:

"Don't kill them."

You remained silent and began closing all the shutters that covered our windows, while mamá, wrapped in sheets, went like a ghost up the stairs, in complete silence. And I stood watching how you closed the shutters of our house, jamming the bars across them, fastening the padlocks, and storing the keys on a large copper ring attached to your black linen pants.

"Go to bed at once, Lucas," you ordered then. And I went up the stairs without taking my eyes off you.

When you had almost finished closing all the shutters, there came an insistent knocking at the front door. The knocking was loud and unrelenting.

"Are we expecting anyone, Esther?"

"No, Señor," she answered, standing in the doorway of the barn where my nursemaids slept.

When you left the house, the women all went to the front door to look. I disobeyed you, running downstairs and slipping like a cat between the skirts of Mara and Sarai, who always smelled of bread. All I could see beyond the gate, far in the distance, were two men on horseback, but it was impossible to make out their features. Esther said she hadn't heard the horses approaching, and Sarai responded that all we ever heard inside the house these days were cows.

I couldn't think of anyone who might arrive at our house on a Sunday night. Even during the week no one came up here, except for Sister Bruna and Father Hetz, who came to administer the Eucharist, and also Professor Erlano, though I couldn't tell you whether he came up or down because we never found out where he lived. The townsfolk only came when we threw a party.

We watched how those men climbed down from their horses and spoke to you for a long while. Then you all began approaching along the cobbled path, turning off toward the stables to leave the animals. When you reappeared, the three of you were talking like old friends. One of them had his hand on your back, father, a hand with the red, misshapen knuckles of an acromegalic.

"Light the candles, bring out fruit and wine. And prepare hot water and dry clothes for these men," you said then to my nurse-maids, coming in through the front door as these two strangers followed in your wake. You didn't seem frightened by those tangled beards, long and filthy, the heavy black clothing, nor by the men's resemblance to a pair of bison with hollows in place of eyes.

Throughout that cold and dusty night, I tossed and turned in bed. I was afraid that if I fell asleep, something would happen, afraid too that if I didn't fall asleep, something would happen. The lowing of the cows had begun to seep into my dreams like smoke, suffusing everything, yet it was sounding more and more tired, as if resigning itself. Until a complete silence enveloped the house. It was a silence I experienced for the first time; though perhaps I'd encountered it once before on emerging from my mother's womb, as any sound would have caused my delicate ears to burst.

The night's silence shook me and spread like a rotten smell, clinging to my body and leaving it mute.

At that moment, I got up and cracked open my bedroom door; it was then that I saw the two men walking behind the wooden columns out front. Their great dirty boots splattered mud as they went, making a splashing sound on the tiled floor.

They were only two, but they sounded like a battalion, and their noise collided with everything around because everything had been touched by that murky silence; everything except for them. The one walking behind had a pronounced hunch, and yet was still just as tall as the other.

On reaching the door, their heads grazed the wooden frame. They inserted the cylindrical key into the door and entered the room across from mine, the one you'd given them, father, so they could sleep peacefully.

The night shuddered.

The cows had ceased their lowing.

Silence reigned, in spite of the noises made by those men as they slept. Or perhaps because of them.

ELOY'S FOOT

Offhand, I can only recall seeing three things in my life that instantly made an impression on me, for better or worse. The first was the wooden leg of Señor Lazlo, head of the funfair that came to town during carnival. I wasn't impressed so much by the wooden leg itself: these were commonplace in our town, after all; rather, it was the meticulously carved ants crawling up the leg that captivated me. They had miniscule amber stones for eyes, symbols of health and happiness explained Señor Lazlo as he walked with those ants, statuettes, trapped on his wooden leg. The second was the day I accidentally walked into my nursemaids' bedroom as Esther, who suffered from sciatica, was receiving a backrub from Mara. She lay stretched out on the bed with her bottom on display to the entire world, a bottom that sagged on either side like oven-ready dough. The third was Eloy's foot.

I saw it on the first morning they awoke inside our house. After being accompanied for so long by the lowing of the cows, we rose swathed in silence, as if the house had filled with voices that whispered: *hide, be quiet, stay still.*

Even after midday, no one dared approach the room where they slept. You, father, had told us only their names: Felisberto and Eloy.

"Give them a good breakfast. They've come a long way!" you yelled, before hurrying off to conduct your business in town, leaving someone else to deal with the consequences of yesterday's Good Samaritan act.

Sarai, Noah, and Mara laughed quietly in the kitchen, glancing at each other as though harboring a girly secret. The presence of those men unsettled them. Esther said that what we'd allowed into the house was a pair of ne'er-do-wells who knew absolutely nothing of manners, seeing as the night before they'd left the dining room a pigsty. My mother was restless and uneasy because no one had consulted her. "I have a bad feeling about this, Lucas. Something smells terrible. Terrible," she whispered in my ear when I went out to see her in the garden. She was busy sowing the last row of wallflowers to crown her grand design: an enormous spiral of flowers that would fill with different colors depending on the month of the year. I wandered from the kitchen to the upper floor and back down to the garden, then started over. I was waiting for the hairy giants to leave their bedroom, my insides squirming with curiosity, but from that room not a sound arrived.

By two in the afternoon, curiosity and anticipation were turning to dread. A wave of fear was passing over all of us, father. I knew it, my mother knew it, Esther knew it, even the plants in the garden knew it: that evening the dandelions all closed before dark. When we sat down to lunch, ready for some pork hock soup, no one spoke. We served each dish slowly: the gristly pork in its broth, the potatoes in their sauce, and the hominy corn in salt. We served it all knowing there were two strangers in the house who might well be dead. Everything smelled good, but no one started eating. Suddenly, Noah began to yell:

"They're coming up the path, they're coming up the path. It's them, the visitors!"

My mother and I crept over to the window and watched them approaching.

"Enough to drive you mad," she said. "They left the house without anybody hearing. It's enough to drive us all mad."

Before coming through the front door, they took off their boots and socks, and it was then that I noticed Eloy's foot. It was covered in scabs, some of which clung to his sock. The foot was peeling like the bark of a *Polylepis*, the paper trees up on the paramo. He appeared to give this no thought and would periodically wipe his foot as though removing fluff, causing pieces of his skin to fall to the ground. He wasn't the least bit ashamed.

When they entered the house, I couldn't take my eyes off the scabbed foot, which hobbled all the way over to my mother. I was so astonished by this sight, I didn't even notice that the other man, Felisberto, was carrying a deer in his arms, a small dead buck.

"Delighted, Señora Torrente." This was all Felisberto said before leaving the deer on the kitchen counter, already beheaded, its legs bound.

As soon as she caught sight of the animal, my mother was sick down the side of her chair. A puny regurgitation: it had been hours since breakfast. She rose and picked up a cloth, with which she began wiping her mouth. Esther tried unsuccessfully to move the deer before Sarai ran over to help, and together they pushed it toward the basin, blood seeping out all over the kitchen counter. Noah followed behind, mopping the floor, while Mara raised her hands to her mouth, repeating, "Oh, little one! What have they done to you?"

The men sat down, untroubled by what had just taken place, and the foot disappeared under the table.

"It was very kind of your husband to take us in, Señora," said Felisberto, with that habit he had of touching his beard as he talked, as though always on the point of saying something very serious.

My mother nodded and tried reluctantly to smile, as she continued to wipe her mouth with the cloth and take deep breaths, still embarrassed about the vomiting incident.

"I'm sorry. It's just that we don't normally eat venison," said mamá, taking my hand under the table.

"But today we shall try it for our guests! One should always be ready to eat new things, to try new things, my dear Josefina," you said, coming in through the front door at that very moment.

My mother looked at you in confusion. Sometimes my mother would look at you as if she woke each day and asked herself "Who is this? And what am I doing here?" That's precisely how she looked at you then, father. And not only her; I too had begun looking at you this way.

"How about preparing a stew, girls? And, my Josefina, why not come through and talk to us. Have you seen my wife yet? One of the more singular specimens, I assure you," you said, looking at Felisberto and Eloy. And you started to laugh.

Mamá asked permission to clean herself

up before joining you, while you guided your guests into the living room and told them of your morning's adventures, your dealings with the traders at the market. "Those people think they can put one over on me, but by the time they get going, gentlemen, I've lapped them twice already," you commented and continued to laugh. You continued to laugh as you began showing them the antique Art Deco table, the chandelier inherited from a great-grandmother, the rug grandfather had brought back from the Old Continent.

"I was almost forgetting, gentlemen, would you care for a cognac or some aguardiente with ice? Choose the aguardiente, for nothing says the good life like caña."

Felisberto nodded for the pair of them, and in under an hour you had polished off an entire bottle between the three of you. You behaved so oddly, were so refined and good-natured, that it frightened me, especially because you seemed estranged from the rest of us. It was as if you only had eyes for them, appearing intent on becoming the best host the world had ever seen. A submissive, docile, and credulous host. And you did not stop behaving like this, father. From that moment forth you carried on in the same way. Day after day. As if you'd always been waiting for those men. As one waits for death.

ASSASSIN BUG

Now that I'm back, father, standing before our house, I see you once again on that cold, dirty night. I see it all again: my nursemaids sitting side-on, with Esther braiding their hair tightly, her hands trembling; my mother looking out of the window, frightened by that sound that was draining us; and you, stood atop the old Bentwood bench: you close the shutters, slide the bars across, fasten the padlocks.

Were you locking us inside your own nightmare?

The day has not yet dawned but the sky is viscous and there is no wind. I cross the garden in five slow, meditative paces. In my mind everything is spinning. It's as though I were no longer seeing through my eyes, as though in place of flesh and viscera I had within me a cold, dense fog. Something, as yet undefined, pulses beneath my skin and drives me on.

The flaking paint on the walls of the house reveals the cracked adobe, and when I lean against it, earth comes crumbling out; the roof, gapped like rows of old rotten teeth, rattles slowly; the shutters screech as they slam against the windows. And I walk because I can no longer drag myself.

With a bit more luck, I could have been a spiny flower mantis, a Hercules beetle, or an assassin bug. If I were an assassin bug, I would scuttle away right now along the ground to what is left of our house and roam all around it without anyone noticing me, causing mischief here and there, clambering up Felisberto and Eloy's bodies, summoning my band of friends to do our work. I would bite their hands, their necks, beneath their buttocks, their thighs, devour their entire bodies, and when I could go on no longer and found myself swollen, obese, filled up with blood, perhaps I would burst from sheer contentment.

But I've had to settle for what I am and

hone my most advantageous skills. When it has proven necessary, I've even learned to lie and steal with no remorse, father. I stole fruit from Señor Elmur, mangos in particular, which I allowed to rot and breed flies, before sharing the putrid peels with the slugs and snails.

Señor Elmur was not deserving of those mangos because he refused to wait for them, forcing me to tear them off while they were still green, unconcerned that my skin became covered in burns and blisters. And I didn't just steal his mangos, but also prickly pears I ate whole, even though I then spent days with invisible spines in my hands, which stung when I put them in my pockets. And, just once, I stole a diseased chicken too, which I allowed to die and decay, and in the folds and furrows of its skin I later cultivated maggots and eventually flies, which swarmed all around me inside that dark hollow in the field where I took refuge, before settling on the rocks and brambles and multiplying.

And what beautiful music could be heard, father, when they were in flight; they were wings and they were life, a hallowed symmetry that whispers.

I would have no problem hanging Felisberto and Eloy from the rafters and wounding their bodies until their flesh turned gangrenous, until they were surrounded by so many flies the buzzing would crack their skulls. I want all this and nothing more, father. I want the resurrection of the flesh that only comes with the end and ordure. Ultimately, all I want is to return, but to return just like that is as impossible as changing myself into a praying mantis, because praying mantises scurry along at a velocity I could never hope to match, though my mind races. Praying mantises scurry, cows ruminate, birds chirp, and my mind races at a rate of words per second, until I collide with all the masses of the universe.

I walk along the porch and the verandas surrounding the house, looking inside the eaves for wasps, for caterpillars of moths or butterflies; in places where the paint is peeling, I peer between the blocks of earth; where there are bricks, I look inside gaps, spy through cracks; that's where my spiders are, my furious weevils, my skilful centipedes. I know they're all inside this house, our house, a scab of dried earth; with its darkness, which is a breeding ground, it has provided them a place to await my return. They are miniscule, beautiful, and loyal.

Sometimes, when I'm in the midst of my meticulous observations, I feel that you, father, enter through some door in my mind and bellow: "Snap out of it, Lucas. Stop moping about like a fool." And I tremble, but it's not a fear that terrifies me. It isn't truly your voice, father, for I can't remember that. Hard as I try, I can only hear those phrases, limp from overuse, that you employed in every situation. But they are echoes. Echoes that expand and take the form I give them.

I am the creator of a father. And it will not be in my image and likeness that he forms in my recollections, but with invented voices, weak articulations, a father who drags himself through my mind: repentant, a prisoner of my memory.

My father. My horror.

When I reach the front door, I knock and do the only thing one can do in a situation like this: something foul. I recall I haven't eaten, slept, or relieved myself in days, that everything has been the return. Since I can do neither the first nor the second, my nervousness compels me to the third. As I detect footsteps approaching the door, heavy footsteps I know well, I also detect the warm urine falling between my thighs. The odor calms me for a moment.

I breathe it in as deeply as I can and fill my heart with ammonia, yet suddenly I feel a weight at the back of my pants. Something drops. Three small stones. Surprise unsettles the bowels. I can't deny that I take pleasure in Felisberto's expression, looking down at me as if I were decomposing, just before I feel the blow to my face. The deformed hand knocks me from my torpor.

The scent of ammonia has disappeared completely. I smell of pond water and my cheek throbs. My return is a sad one. Only the hairy giant receives me. They are forcing me to become angry. Where are the women now that I've returned, father? There is no trace of anyone.

No one does right by the orphan. Under

these circumstances, for a moment, I am like a castigating god. I am like that selfsame God of the Old Testament, though less blood-thirsty, for I have no desire to extinguish the planet, an act that led God to become so lonely and miserable he felt compelled to divide himself in three: Father, Son, and the Holy Spirit (this last the most tiresome of all and good for absolutely nothing).

He ended up alone because he destroyed men, because he had observed that their wickedness was great and wanted to remake all he had created, like a boy displeased with his clay figurines; he saw them as formless, always unfinished, and felt regret and fury, and yet sometimes it was better when God acted in this way, for afterwards he would lose even the desire to play with and destroy figurines, instead leaving them to rot.

But God did not know what I know; God did not know how to teach man to decompose, to relinquish his voice and his words, liquefy his insides, rise up and escape from his man's body, which is only a pupa.

Hallowed music, hallowed melody that whispers.

THE MILKING

By the third day the whole house smelled of rancid raisins. Exuding from Felisberto and Eloy's room came that fruity smell, perhaps even a little rotten, but a scent one wanted to follow for its sweetness. When I woke up, I peered out at them through the window. They were milking the cows. Their hands were so large the udders disappeared inside their grasp. And I saw them drink the thick, unblemished milk like two beasts, taking turns with the bucket.

I was coming down the stairs when they entered our house with the dawn light at their backs. They closed the door with an authority that led me to believe they would no longer be leaving, or at least this was what I felt, because premonitions exist and that must have been the first I'd ever had:

Felisberto and Eloy would not be leaving, father.

"Want milk?" Felisberto asked me, laughing, as I watched him cross the hall in long strides, the other following like his shadow. I looked at him fearfully and fled to the kitchen, where Esther was washing grapefruits. Noah and Mara were making compote and you were sitting at the old table, squeezed into your linen pajamas with those bright red stripes, the ones that buttoned up to your neck. At the table where the fruit was normally chopped and the meat pounded, you, father, were drinking coffee with an air that struck me as utterly ridiculous.

At that moment, I looked everywhere, looked at Esther, Noah, and Mara, as if wanting to warn them: here they come! But they, the visitors, were already there. No matter how fast I ran, their long legs always outstripped me.

"We brought milk," said Felisberto, and Eloy followed behind him, carrying the buckets without the least bit of care, jowls trembling, leaving a trail of white droplets like murky rain.

I wasn't sure whether Eloy was mute or an idiot, but if one strained one's ears, it was just possible to make out a soft groan coming from his mouth. It was as though he were constantly moaning, like a man made of despair, wheezing, and whispers: *hide, be quiet, stay still.*

Noah and Mara abandoned the half-filled jars of plum compote and went about serving four glasses of fresh milk. They set them down on the table. "Your drinks, gentlemen," said Mara, and Noah laughed mischievously. They served Felisberto and Eloy first, then you, father, and, last of all, me. Ever since their arrival, I was always served last.

"You're early risers," you said to them, as you mixed your preserved figs into the fresh quesillo. "I'm pleased. I'm ever so pleased! Good habits are of the utmost importance. They deliver man from misfortune. But that is of no concern right now. Tell me, my good men, have you considered what we spoke of yesterday?"

Felisberto made no reply until he had finished his glass of milk, holding it suspended between his mouth and the table as he watched Noah's swaying hips, Noah, who at that moment was softly humming something resembling the "Wedding March" and carrying on with the compotes. You looked at her too, and smiled. Felisberto put the glass down heavily and wiped his palm across his mouth.

"We won't charge you a thing for the labor. All we ask is that you allow us to stay until the beginning of the harvest. In March, we'll leave."

"Splendid. I think that's splendid."

"If we could have use of another room, we would be most grateful."

"You can use the one next door to yours. We'll bring in a bed and remove the piano."

"That won't be necessary, Eloy plays the piano. We didn't know you had one. He finds it very calming in the evenings."

"Calming?"

"It makes him sleepy."

"In days gone by, it was my mother who played the piano. Oh, my mother! She had the slenderest of fingers, the skin almost imperceptible. When she played piano, you would hear the sound of her bones on the keys before the note even reached you. Bone on ..."

"God have mercy!" cried Sarai at that moment from the second floor of the house, where, judging by the sound and time of day, she must have been sweeping.

Felisberto looked surprised, but not entirely.

"Don't worry, gentlemen. The women in this house are always impatient, always fussing about something or other. Sometimes they say they hear footsteps, voices; other times they cry out because the washing flies unaided from the clothesline into the sky. And they say this is spirits. They call even the wind a spirit. The word *calamity* was invented for these women."

Felisberto nodded. "Bloody women!" he said humorlessly, and with something akin to repugnance, but not entirely. And you burst into laughter.

Eloy's demeanor remained unchanged. He drank from his glass of milk with a hypnotic vulgarity. Streaming down either side of his face were tiny white rivulets, which he would wipe away with the edge of the tablecloth when they reached his neck. The liquid followed the line of his dirty black hair, which was parted in the middle and fell like waves about his beard. He hadn't washed it since he'd arrived at the house; or, to judge by its appearance, perhaps it had never been washed at all.

I left the three of them to their chatter and went in search of Sarai. When I reached the second floor, I found her in the little card-playing room, leaning out of the window. I promptly peered out and spotted what had given her such a fright. The cows were wandering in circles through my mother's garden. They were tearing up the wallflowers and sweet alyssums; the red and amber seed pods of Chinese lanterns were hanging from their snouts. They then crammed these into their mouths with their large jaws and mashed them. It was like watching the cows gorge themselves sick on sweets.

Soon they settled down onto the ground, lowering their bodies slowly but inexorably, first the hind legs, then the fore. They lay still, as though their gluttony had filled them with remorse.

"Mamá," I cried out at that moment.

For just then my mother had surfaced from her room, her angel hair looking exactly like a nest of fine noodles, only darker. It was so fine, in fact, that I imagined as an old woman her head would be left covered in nothing but fluff. She was wearing her long petticoats, still trailing her slumber.

"Mother! Don't come out here. Go back in your room," I implored.

But my mother, drowsy as she was, did what any person does when they're told not to turn and look. She went over and leaned out of the window. She stood there, staring. From the kitchen came the sound of your laughter and that of those men, as my mother stared down at the cows lying in her garden, chewing flowers, snapping stalks, and treading on clover with a passivity that felt grotesque. And the sound of your laughter, father, must have swept over everything she saw.

Before I knew it, mamá had put her boots on and was heading down the stairs in an unexpected fit of rage. Her eyes were blank. It was like watching a landslide. Something had shifted, and heaps of stone had started to break away and tumble downwards. Toward an abyss.

When I saw her next, she was racing up the stairs with one of the rifles you kept in the cellar, her petticoats flouncing with every step.

Without a moment's hesitation, she aimed out of the window.

The cow was already lying on the ground, so the bullet simply caused it to bow its head and groan, almost imperceptibly. Your laughter downstairs stopped. You and Felisberto came straight up the stairs. You found Sarai and me standing in a corner, not sure what had happened. We looked at my mother, who at that moment had sunk to the floor, as though kneeling, but with her legs parted and the rifle between them, a minaret among the petticoats. She began to weep disconsolately.

And then you grabbed hold of her firmly and I wanted you to let her go.

"Josefina!"

My mother failed to wake from her trance and you shook her even more vigorously by the shoulder.

"Josefina! Josefina!"

My mother cried and wiped her eyes, unable to control the shallow gasps that punctuated her weeping.

"The wallflowers were blooming," she said, between sobs.

"Go call Esther, Lucas. Tell her to prepare something for your mother. Something strong ... and to fetch Father Hetz," you said, looking into my eyes as though you had only just realized that I was there and was your son.

"I'll fetch him myself," said Sarai, who had crouched down to stroke my mother's hair and try to calm her sobbing.

At that moment, Felisberto came over too, and grabbed my mother by the other arm. As they tried to lift her, Felisberto addressed her slowly, and in a manner that appeared courteous, but wasn't entirely.

"Perhaps you're in need of some rest, Señora Torrente."

"Let go of me," said my mother. "Let me go! What are you still doing here?"

"It's none of your concern, Josefina. They'll be staying a little longer. They're working

with me. You know how long I've spent looking for someone to assist me."

"They can't stay. This is not their home."

"Be quiet. I have no desire to listen to you
right now. These men are willing to help me."

"But what are you still doing here, Lucas?"
you turned to say to me. "Run and see Esther."

Sarai took my hand and together we went
downstairs, where Esther stood waiting
alongside Noah and Mara. Esther would not
stop crossing herself and murmuring what
was surely another Hail Mary from the
infinite rosary she never ceased reciting.

"We didn't go up so as not to disturb.
What's happened to Señora Josefina? How
easy it is to become lost without God."

"Hush, Esther. It was an accident," Sarai
told her.

"With God there are no accidents."

"Hush now. Go make some linden tea, and
throw in a bit of cognac. And let's have no
more talking." Her eyes widened angrily as
she said this.

"Come here, Lucas, and help us with these
compotes," said Noah and Mara. "Later, we'll
give you a bath. Then we can go apple pick-

ing. We've seen trees covered in apples, haven't wc, Sarai?"

"Yes," said Sarai, "we'll go see about those apples. That'll be the best plan for today."

We all went back to the kitchen and Esther busied herself preparing the linden tea, while Sarai left to fetch Father Hetz.

Eloy didn't even turn to watch us come in. None of what had happened mattered to him. He finished his milk and rose slowly, white lagoons crisscrossing his filthy beard, that same appalling groan he always let out when he moved.

We saw him leave and then appear again outside, heading toward the garden. He kicked the cow lying on the ground and it didn't move, although the cloud of flies around it scattered upwards and disappeared. After confirming the cow was no longer living, Eloy left it in the middle of the garden. He stuck his fingers in his mouth and whistled. The other cows came over to him, and he began walking toward the pen. The cows followed in a docile line.

THE PIANO

Sarai was the youngest of all the girls and was missing the index and middle fingers of her left hand. When she took my hand, she would squeeze too tightly with the three remaining fingers, her grip like that of a riled hen. But this was the only rough gesture she had to offer. Sometimes, it seemed to me that the hand did not belong to her, that it was a false hand she would one day remove, to be replaced with the hand of a newborn child. I imagined us watching it grow for years, until it matched the other.

I would think about things like this whenever I walked along beside Sarai, which is why I used to stumble into every ditch; I'd fall on the ground, usually onto my backside, and she would pick me back up again using her chicken foot. We were like a poorly oiled

bicycle chain—advancing in fits and starts.

I held onto her hand, the bad one, as we went to pick those blessed apples. Noah and Mara walked ahead of us, with that very long hair they let down as soon as they left the house. They unwound the tight braids Esther forced them to wear and undid the top buttons of their starched smock uniforms, until they resembled a pair of flying nymphs. They were laughing about something we couldn't hear.

Although Sarai was the youngest of all the girls, she behaved more seriously, the false older sister. Or perhaps it was that Noah and Mara were like those couples who leave no room for anyone else, having spent an eternity together.

We crossed the garden and saw the enormous body of the cow lying in the grass, surrounded by miniscule flies, reminding us that something had taken place back at the house; yet, as we passed it, we all looked the other way.

We walked along the path until we reached the fruit trees, but instead of picking apples, we sat down and took off our shoes. The sun beat down gently on our faces and from time to time allowed a warm breeze to tickle the whole of our bodies.

For a second, that light made me forget what had happened with my mother. I forgot that Felisberto and Eloy were at the house. It was one of those moments when we turn back time without meaning to. I lay in the grass for a long while, belly up, wondering if all those shiny specks that appear in the sky when we look directly at the sun were pieces of other worlds.

When I felt the sun begin to burn my cheeks, I turned over and started dragging myself along like a reptile, observing the skylarks balancing on the lowest branches of the apple trees, like miniature trapeze artists. I advanced slowly so as not to startle them, but Noah's laughter, that shrill laughter, drove them off. Noah was laughing incessantly, while Mara sang a little song:

Peppers green, blue and red,
Señorita X wants to be wed.
And she won't say
who her boyfriend is.
It's Señorito X.

Noah could not stop laughing. She laughed to the point of screeching, like a marmot. I swear it was like a marmot.

"He loves me, he loves me not, he loves me, he loves me not. The daisies will tell us."

Mara continued to sing as she pulled up the purple shamrocks that abounded among the grass, scattered like stray brush strokes. The larger shamrocks resembled gigantic butterflies. My mother adored them. Mara plucked off leaf after leaf and then flung the stems away, filled with euphoria.

Sarai raised her head and glared, as though wishing to petrify the girls, but Mara interrupted her.

"The truth is, you could marry him far more easily than either of us could."

"What are you talking about!" hissed Sarai.

"We've seen how he looks at you. Though today I caught him looking at me too, and it's made me burst into song."

I listened attentively to this quiet chatter, and didn't like it one bit. Neither did Sarai. She lay down again on the flat expanse and closed her eyes, as if this would allow her to stop listening.

"If Esther knew, she'd go crazy," said Noah, "if she knew the things you say. Oh! She can be so bitter."

"She wasn't like that before. But perhaps I understand her. When a woman gets old, even her guts must wrinkle up inside her."

This statement was greeted by more shrieks of laughter.

"That's enough now!" said Sarai, angrily. "A person can't even lie down in peace without having to listen to your nonsense. There's no peace with the two of you. You're like a pair of parakeets! Silly, tiresome parakeets. It would take a deaf person to put up with you—a deaf old crone. Come on, Lucas, let's go pick those apples!"

I left the apple picking to them, instead retrieving a stick we'd brought along with us and beginning to ride on it. For a moment, I imagined they were three damsels in distress, and that someone was chasing after them; from my white horse, which I was able to steer even with no hands, I took out my gun and fired. "Bang! Bang!" I cried.

Sarai became even more annoyed.

"Enough, Lucas! Come here and help me."

But I paid her no attention and began catching grasshoppers. Green grasshoppers, greener than anything I'd ever seen, even in the most vibrant watercolor. I slipped them into my pocket to show my mother.

We returned home before nightfall, all four of us engulfed in a deep silence, with four baskets full of apples. Mine was heavy, but I carried it with just one hand, as the other was keeping the grasshoppers trapped inside my pocket. Esther, who was waiting at the door, took the baskets off us one by one, overflowing with delight.

"We'll make a pie!" she exclaimed.

"How is Señora Josefina?" Sarai asked, gravely.

"Sleeping. They've given her something to make her sleep."

As soon as we crossed the threshold, we heard it. The music coming from the piano filled the entire house, which was revealed, for the first time, to have an echo. The piano could be heard in the kitchen and the living room and the bedrooms, and if one travelled into town, it would surely be possible to hear it there as well, with shocking clarity. As though the piano were everywhere.

"Señor Eloy is playing the piano," said Esther. "He's quite the talent."

Then she left the apples in the kitchen and we all went to watch Eloy play. It really was captivating. He was a circus gorilla, tamed, playing a Brahms sonata. You were sitting behind him, alongside Felisberto, drinking aguardiente. I went over to you, and a grasshopper escaped from my pocket onto your legs.

"What are you doing?! Get those bugs out of here! Christ on the cross, this obsession with bugs, Lucas!"

The grasshopper sprang onto the piano and stayed there for a moment, alive but motionless.

Noah and Mara sat down beside you and Felisberto. I backed slowly into a corner, where Sarai stood staring intently at the ground.

"I want to see my mother, Sarai."

"Go on, little one."

"Aren't you coming with me?"

"Not now. I'd like to listen for a while."

I left you all there and went to see my

mother. As I moved away, I saw all of you as if inside a painting, one of those paintings from formal dining rooms in large houses that overshadow everything around them, because no one in those pictures is really looking back at us.

And I began to loathe you all, father. You most of all.

Because I understand now that all fathers have a god inside them and look down upon their sons like clay figurines, always incomplete, wanting to create them over and over in their own image and likeness. And these fathers condemn their sons: they send plagues and floods, they issue curses, before eventually forgiving them for their own vanity. And all men on earth are nothing but cracked and timorous clay sons who wander through life, now missing an arm, now a leg, now deformed. Yet nobody sees us.

SQUISHY WHITE LARVA

I look sidelong at the giant. My body trembles, but not with fear. I'm feverish. For a long time, I've wanted to be here, in this moment, in front of Felisberto, inside this house which is ours. To grovel and plead to be taken back.

I wanted to humiliate myself, to kiss his hand, gigantic and hairy, to be his servant, the most loyal in the world, the kind who, upon realizing the one they serve is despicable, force themselves to love him even more. I wanted it with all my heart, father. Then I understood you. A person can become infatuated with the monstrous. I remember how I once watched a small boy approach Señor Elmur's farm. He was a boy with a clear gaze, father. He had the look of a child the entire world would want to embrace.

When he drew near, he begged me to give him something: food, blankets, anything.

I gave him a kick to the knees, because who was he to approach me? Why ask me for protection, if I myself had nothing?

But each day he came back, father. He came asking for food and bedding, only to be rewarded each day with another one of my kicks. He'd grab hold of his shin, hopping up and down on one foot.

Whenever I felt completely alone, as alone as a clay figurine inside an oven, as alone as a beetle inside an egg that never hatches, all I wanted was to return to this house. And take a kicking.

I wanted to watch them, continue spying. Ever since they sent me away from here, I've found myself impelled each day to return, to slip into their lives, breathe their obscene air, sleep listening to their brutish snoring, feel their footsteps, walk with them, smell what they leave behind along with their sweat: live among their dead skin, which is ours.

I don't know why these feelings should seem so repulsive. When fly larvae are ready to be born, everything they are liquifies inside their pupae and forms something entirely different: a fly. Pointed legs and geometrically sculpted wings emerge from a squishy white larva.

The same happens with what I feel; everything inside me undergoes a metamorphosis, and even the most repugnant feeling can transform into a prodigious idea, if I so wish.

But I don't want to get ahead of myself; let's leave the repugnance to swarm around me.

Isn't that what you taught me?

After the blow, Felisberto looks at me for several minutes, then laughs with that sardonic laugh of his as he talks and strokes his beard. He's sitting on the front doorstep, removing gunk from under his fingernails before chewing them off and spitting them at me.

"What the hell are you doing here, you little wretch?"

I stand tall and puff out my chest.

"Little? Really? Take a good look."

He rises, as though losing patience, and paces around me. He's about to deal the second blow. I step back, accept one of his murderous looks and kneel with my hands pressed together at my chest.

Felisberto pushes the door open with his foot and calls to Eloy, who drags himself outside with his stiff leg, which he lifts as if it were a wooden limb. Eloy goes to the barrel of rainwater and brings over a full basin. He merely groans, but I hear: *hide, be quiet, stay still*.

"Take off your pants," says Felisberto. I do this and Eloy pours the water over me, then allows the basin to fall on me.

"My Lord. I have returned for your sake. You are all I have left. Sarai, Noah, Mara, and you. When a person has been forced to grovel to eat, how can they continue to live far from home?" I ask them.

"Get up off the ground," he orders. "How could that greedy old man let you go?"

"I escaped. I poisoned him. But there is no danger, it wasn't lethal. Hydrangea tea doesn't kill in such small doses. Soon, he'll crawl from the outhouse and it's possible he'll come for me, but don't let him, my Lord, don't let him take me," I implore, as I pull on my wet and dirty pants, so wet, I have to hold them up with my hands.

"To hell with that. I'm not returning what he paid for you."

"If I work here, I can pay him back myself. Look at me, look at my arms, ready to haul, look at my chest, strong as an ox. I'll do whatever you ask, so long as you let me stay. I'll work night and day until my bones ache in my sleep, and even my dreams will be bitter if you so desire."

"Don't get smart. I won't have a liar working for me."

"Master—may I call you that?—Señor Elmur was always asking about my father. He found it all very strange, bizarre even. 'Something smells rotten,' he would say. 'Tell me,' he would plead at night, 'what did you see? What happened? Why do you tremble?' 'I can help you,' he would offer, over and over. And he'd give me chicken skin to eat if I told him something, he'd give me the skin and not just stale bread."

"Shut your mouth, you snivelling brat."

"He said my father's lands should not be left in the hands of strangers, that something needed to be done. And I didn't betray you. Oh no, my Lord, I'd sooner be dead. Well and truly dead."

"To hell with Elmur, he's an even bigger shit than you are."

"I'm sorry, Master. I've upset you. Let me stay, I beg you. I beg you. I'm cold, I'm hungry."

A BURNT OFFERING

Father Hetz arrived along with Sister Bruna, weighed down with hosts for administering the Eucharist to us. Sister Bruna carried hosts by the dozen, wrapped in silk handkerchiefs, spread across her pockets and her handbag; who knows how many times a day she took the host in secret, convinced it was the body of the Lord, but filled with a pure and sacred gluttony.

I had a certain fascination with Sister Bruna, with her chaste scent, not even masked beneath the scent of soap, with her black veil, which never creased and which she moved like a schoolgirl flicking her ponytail, with her secret legs and their divine and bony ankles, peeking out sockless beneath her habit, and with the fine gold anklet and its pendant of St. Simeon Stylites.

Her shoes never bore so much as a smudge, and were small and very narrow, as if Sister Bruna's feet were made of glass. She made a person want to behave impiously in her presence, to tear off her shoes and kiss her feet and caress her ankles until God himself came down to punish them, a punishment that would be sweet and well-deserved.

They arrived accompanied by two women from the town, devout and genteel, but as horrid as parsley, their hair gathered at the base of their necks and their lips painted a pastel pink.

After administering communion to us, father, they shut themselves in the study with you, not reemerging until late in the afternoon, when Felisberto and Eloy arrived.

"Would you like to take communion, Señores?" asked Father Hetz.

"Yes, Father," replied Felisberto.

"*In nomine Patris, et Filii, et Spiritus Sancti. Amen.*"

It was only Felisberto who received the Eucharist, standing with his hands behind his back. Father Hetz had to climb up onto the green ottoman to reach his mouth.

"May we see Señora Josefina now?" asked Father Hetz.

In that moment I wasn't sure why they wanted to see my mother. Had I known, I would have bitten their legs, like some rabid dog ready to infect them, plunging my fangs deep into their flesh, causing them both pain and fright, even Sister Bruna, especially Sister Bruna, for what they were about to do.

"I've told you about everything, even the books," you said to Felisberto.

"What books, father?" I came over to ask you, having been playing under the stairs.

You didn't answer me. You didn't even look at me, father.

Then, Eloy, who'd been sitting on the sofa scratching his legs, rose and picked me up like a cat that needed to be taken outside to prevent it peeing in the living room. I smelled his rotten torso, his clothes impregnated with filthy sweat. I beat him with my childish fists. As I went, I saw the horrid women watching me in delight, smiles appearing behind those vulgar pink lips, because pun-

ishments pleased them, the violence of a jus-
tified hiding.

We stayed outside for a long time, Eloy
grunting as he toyed with the ants. He killed
scores of them, one by one, until his index
finger was covered in a black mass of wrecked
exoskeletons, then he licked it as if it were
honey.

I bawled like an idiot, watching this great
miniscule massacre.

I tried to get up. Again and again, it was
enough for him to simply grab me by the
ankle or the leg with his apelike hand to
force me to remain seated by his side. Very
still, tired of waiting.

Suddenly, you all came pouring out. Sarai,
Noah, Esther, Mara, the horrid women, Sister Bruna, Father Hetz, and you walking
ahead of the rest, bearing books and papers,
engravings and pages of all sizes, large al-
bums you carried without the least bit of
care, allowing pressed leaves and flowers to
drop out. At that precise moment, I understood what was happening.

You were holding everything my mother
kept inside the chest from Cundinamarca.

That chest had belonged to her uncle Enrique, the one who went missing, and had arrived along with a final letter from Cundinamarca. After that, and in order to avoid the pain of continuing to search for him, the family had decided to declare him dead, and my mother was left with the chest, which she referred to from then on as the Cundinamarca Chest. It was inside this chest that she kept all her books on botany, her engravings, the insects of Jan van Kessel the Elder, growing guides, herbal remedies, grimoires, entomological books: the secrets of her world.

Ever since I was little, I had spent entire afternoons by her side looking at those books with their hard, worn-leather covers, fascinated by the indexes, which I thought of as roll calls of women from distant kingdoms: *Araucaria excelsa*, *Chamaedorea elegans*, *Eruca sativa*.

I saw you all walk over to where the wallflowers had once been. You piled all your booty in the middle of the stone statues and set fire to it.

You destroyed it, father. You killed the

words, the illustrations, the paper, insect cities, entire forests, secret gardens, everything like a burnt offering, an offering to the god you all admired and before whom you, Father Hetz, and Felisberto crossed yourselves like his most faithful servants, a ghastly trinity. Father Hetz looked at each of the books, examining them like dangerous animals, peering inside, but not approving of any, slamming them shut and shaking his head, denying them their existence. Then he passed them on to you, father, and you tossed them on the fire, the flames rising higher and higher up into the sky.

I saw my mother's world reduced to a pile of rubble, a place no one could ever reconstruct. Still sitting there, I sobbed and hiccupped as I watched you all, with Eloy slobbering like an idiot while he continued to grip me by the ankle.

I saw Felisberto, huge as a giant. Surrounding him, were you, father, Sister Bruna, Father Hetz, my nursemaids, who I'd loved so dearly, and, beside them, the women as horrid as parsley. You resembled a flock of mutilated sheep, with no eyes and only half an ear, a crippled flock staring at the sky around the fire.

God was made in your image and likeness.

CYCLOPS

When I open the door to the room next to the stables, I discover a bench covered in piled-up saddles, saddles you used, saddles belonging to my grandfather, my great-grandfather, one on top of another, old, nibbled on by rats. It's like opening a tomb to find it full of corpses dressed in torn, rotting clothing. I close the door, remove the saddles one by one with a certain solemnity, as if bidding them all farewell, and lie down.

This is my new place: a cell, a tower, a ship, a tunnel. Whatever I want it to be, it will be.

The snorting of the horses that live in the stables next door bothers me. They're Felisberto and Eloy's horses, large and black, devoid of any meekness; their manes, chopped flat, are thick and stiff, their nostrils so wide I could fit my fist inside them, their fetlocks bushy. The yellowish whites of their eyes look singed, and are constantly trained on some far-off point; those horses cannot look at a man, because they would reveal his death to him. They are the horses that Felisberto and Eloy were riding when they arrived, and the horses would never allow us to approach without kicking up a fuss, bashing at the stable doors with snorts of desperation.

Perhaps the horses were ashamed to serve them.

Forgive them, father. They knew not what they did.

From the house, Felisberto allowed me to take nothing but a branched candelabra holding three old white candles, with deformities at their tips, like mounds of snow at the Antarctic. The Antarctic is the only place I can name where I know for certain there is snow. It's the southernmost point existing on Earth, that's what Professor Erlano would say, during one of our classes every Tuesday and Thursday, when he arrived smelling of patchouli. I know all about mythology, about Greece and Rome, about botany and biology, but if you asked me what the world is like today, I would have no idea. I'm alone on my island of ancient history. I never learned anything more about snow, nor about that place so southerly it made me think that beyond it a person could end up falling into space, father. Sometimes I ask myself about things I have no answers for and then make up the answers.

What happens to the wax of an extinguished candle?

Where does it go?

It turns into nightmares, after dark.

Nightmares like a fine mist that gets in through the ears.

The branched candelabra is my new family tree. A sort of mother-candle, father-candle, sibling-candle, which I hold over my entire body to warm myself, before resting it on the edge of the bed, where the heat encircles my toes. There is something inside me since I returned. I feel there is this *other* inside me, father, who appeared when Felisberto allowed me to stay and when I set foot inside this house again; this other who has begun to manifest in the space between my heart and stomach. Perhaps I became this other when I began nearing the house again, as I returned. Or perhaps it was long before I decided to do so.

This thing they call the sternum is beginning to swell, and I can feel how my other settles there.

I remain sprawled out for a long time, and then the door opens, but no light enters; night has fallen. In the candlelight, three pairs of broad hips are slowly revealed, growing even larger, one after the other, as shadows on the wall, before disappearing as they approach and kneel at the foot of the bench. They smell of onion, rosemary, parsley, and turmeric. The icy touch of five hands and a chicken's foot come to rest on my legs, and I know that it's them.

They've come to see me, father.

They touch my navel and my chest, squeeze my ribs. Their hands search for marks, scars. I'm like a child lost through carelessness, a little creature they must gently probe to find out if he's hurt himself, and if the damage is permanent. If I've lost a leg, if I'm all skin and bones, if there are wounds that will never heal.

I keep my mouth shut and hold my breath for long stretches, hoping they might think I'm dead. But they have a way of touching that is disarming, confusing.

My new being falls away like a cloak and I become an orphan once again, and in my helplessness I would surrender even to hyenas, provided they kept me warm.

I sit up and rest my back against the wall behind my bed, my bench, and their hands recoil in fright, all at once. I lean forward, kneeling to reach the candelabra, and begin to illuminate their faces slowly, as if taking part in some dark ritual. Mara and Noah have let their hair down; it falls in waves, gleaming black veils that stick to their temples, their cheeks, their necks, before following the curve of their breasts, revealed by the undone top buttons of their starched smock uniforms, and continuing to fall all the way down to the ground, where it may well turn into a heap of black snakes, penning me in.

They have dark circles under their eyes, hollows of sorrow. Their faces are so pale, wan, and bony that their fleshy lips bulge more than ever, throbbing, as if storing all their blood. When the light reaches Sarai, I look at her face. Examine it.

She is as beautiful as the flower of a carnivorous plant, a Venus flytrap with its tiny filaments like fairy fingers; a beauty that verges on the monstrous, luring you in. She is as beautiful as the red spots on a desert cicada.

Yet even more so.

I rest the candelabra on the table beside me. Noah and Mara now allow their heads to slump forward onto my legs, their hair brushing against me: black snakes. I've never known them so quiet; they were always talking, if not one, then the other, sometimes both at the same time, but now I can even hear their breathing, like that of sleeping children: shallow and warm.

A drop of wax falls onto the metal base, their bony knees knock against the floor at the slightest movement, and the horses' snorting persists like the enduring sound of the sea.

Sarai leans toward me, with something akin to fear, but which isn't entirely. She seems astonished, as if worried I might spring at her. She's so close to me now that her eyes converge and she resembles a cyclops, a freshwater cyclops, its pair of eyes fused together thousands of years ago.

The cyclopes of mythology were giants with a diabolical temperament, something truly unique, explained Professor Erlano, who loved Polyphemus in spite of his saber-like fangs, bushy beard, and pointed ears; perhaps he even loved him because of these things, and would describe the cyclops with such precision that he managed to communicate an ugliness every bit as sublime as the picture he held in his imagination. It's from these creatures that the cyclops found near the surface of rivers derive their name; they are arthropods, like my clearwing moths, wasps, and alderflies. Yet cyclops live in water, theirs is another kingdom. They have no gills, nor— I'm certain of this—do they have a heart. When faced with danger, they coat themselves in eggs as impenetrable as stones, and can live in the most contaminated water, in green and dirty water, trapped in the filth.

They are shamelessly perseverant.

One by one I blow out the candles and violently separate the heads of these other two women, who are beginning to develop pointed ears and a single monstrous eye themselves. They are cyclopes; all three are cyclopes with serpent hair and, if I allow them to, they will sink their fangs into me.

I would like to cry out, father, like a maniac, with thick, hoarse cries emanating from my dry and dirty larynx, release my pent-up cries, violently preserved. I would like to shake my head right now like a madman, and for my cries to be unending. I have cries within my sternum, and yet, it is not me who controls them, but that other inside me who squeezes my lungs so I howl, grunt, and low, just as the cows lowed without knowing why they did so or when they would stop.

I push away their cyclops heads and turn over, curling up into a ball, to protect myself from having to look at them any longer.

I lie stiff and tight as a cocoon and I snarl. All is dark, father. The cyclopes have gone. All that remains is the snorting of the horses, which offends me.

I go outside and wander through the garden until I find a patch of earth in which to dig a hole, a cradle. I roll around and wallow in the dirt, letting out a sigh of intense pleasure. The earth calms my body, my heart multiplies. Ten hearts, that's how many earthworms have. They, too, drag themselves along in the dirt. I roll about until my knees and elbows start to bleed, until I harm this skin that isn't mine. I eat roots and dry grass, swallow all I can, and feel nauseous. The roots nourish and then expel me: such is being born. I want to liquify my insides, forget my language, become tangled in words, and leave this body.

Here lies a prince in his defiled kingdom.

GOD MEDDLES WITH ME

It was always the same. On days when Noah cleaned the furniture, Esther swept and mopped the floor. And I would hide among the white linen curtains, watching the world through a filter that allowed me to see the dust as if it were particles of light. And I'd say: I see God, right now I can see God. And Esther would yell at me to stop behaving like a clown, that I would ruin the linen with my great dirty hands, and to keep quiet. But I knew what really bothered her was that I was meddling with God, that I'd taken his name in vain. Well, God meddled with me all the time, father.

It was on the orders of Father Hetz, his representative on Earth, that my mother was confined to the back of the house. There, all the doors and windows were bricked up. It had been Felisberto and Eloy who took charge of opening up one of the rooms. They spent three whole days removing bricks and ferrying furniture to and fro until they'd prepared a room, with a bed and a bedside table and absolutely nothing else, for my mother to sleep in. "What she needs is a place that imparts tranquillity. The world God left within our reach was not created to be questioned and investigated, but to be contemplated." This is what Father Hetz said to you over a steaming mug of naranjillado laced with aguardiente.

When they'd finished with the renovations and I caught a glimpse of the room where they planned to install my mother, I realized that what Father Hetz, Esther, and you, father, meant by "tranquillity" was in fact pure sorrow. For the first time, I understood why those paintings in which saintly men and women sink down at the foot of a bed to pray filled me with such desolation, when they were intended to inspire joy.

God's tranquillity was a damned empty room.

Our house, which was already large,

suddenly transformed into something as big as an abbey, as big as a nave, immense, and divided into its altar, naves, and towers. Places we had rarely visited began to exist with their own odors, sounds, and apparitions. Do you remember the house well, father? Listen closely, because that house no longer exists. Until that day, our house could have been described as a manor, though I'd always thought of it as a castle. Coming in through the front door, a little to the right, you had the living room, dining room, and kitchen; to the left was your study: the dark tower.

Behind this was the central courtyard, its marble floor covered in clay pots that held an incredible array of succulents. It was framed by large oak columns that led to the bedrooms: mine, the barn where my nursemaids slept, and the rooms you'd given to Felisberto and Eloy. A staircase next to my room climbed from the courtyard up to the second floor, which is where we had the card room and the master bedroom—until that day shared by you and my mother—comprised, in actual fact, of two rooms separated by a large bathroom. It was here that she had washed during the day, and you at night. Further on was the small sitting room with its armchairs, radio, and books; and the little ironing room, also used for siestas, where you allowed Esther, Noah, and Mara (because Sarai never did any ironing) to listen to music on an old gramophone.

Is that right, father? Or have I mixed something up? In any case, this is how the house wishes me to remember it.

Coming off the courtyard was that small iron door that led to the narrow corridor, almost never used. I imagined it as some kind of dungeon. Along it, you could reach another part of the house, with a wall backing onto the stables. That's where *the aunts'* rooms had been, but it could easily have accommodated a whole other family.

The aunts appeared to have no names; they were simply *the aunts*. You never wanted to talk about them. But Esther had told Mara, who told Noah, who one night told me (much to Sarai's irritation) that long ago a rumor had spread that, under cover of darkness, *the aunts* used to escape into town to go dancing with the seminarists.

My great-grandfather had been so horri-
fied by the rumors that he built those rooms,
almost an entire house, just for these women.
But it was a house with no way out, with
thick walls, and that corridor the only means
of escape. And that's where he installed the
iron door, with bolts and padlocks for which
only he had the key. From this part of the
house, looking out through round openings
like mouseholes, you could see nothing but
the hills, which to *the aunts* must have come
to resemble an image of hell. I've never been
able to discover how long they lived there, or
their names, and, come to think of it, I don't
even know how many they were; yet during
those nights when you were all preparing to
move my mother there, father, I imagined
them still locked up inside their rooms,
pleading to be let out.

It was in this part of the house, where the
doors and windows had been bricked up,
that my mother slept, night after night, once
you and God decided it should be so.

After Felisberto and Eloy had finished fix-
ing up the room, Mara and Noah tidied it.
Esther, for her part, took it upon herself to

place a bible and candle on the bedside table, while Sarai positioned a vase of wallflowers to one side. You almost never visited that room, father. Occasionally, you'd come to oversee the entire project, but you passed through quickly, as though the place had a strange effect on you.

During those three days, I'd convinced myself that the final transfer would never take place. For one reason or another, I told myself, you'd see sense and leave my mother where she was. But on the morning Sarai left the vase of wallflowers, I knew the thing you'd all been planning would go ahead, and I ran to your study.

"You're not sending my mother there."

"You're a child, you understand nothing."

"You ..."

"Lower your voice."

"You're blind."

"Get out, Lucas!"

"Blind and crazy!"

"Out! Impudent child."

"I'm not leaving until you promise that my mother isn't moving to that room."

I repeated this with my eyes closed and

hands over my ears. I said it many times, thousands of times, kicking and screaming. I continued to scream it as I began hurling the things inside your study; a quill and inkwell you never used, not that it mattered, papers, papers, two ashtrays, a glass of aguardiente, papers, accounting ledgers, keys, more papers. You, father, had never hit me before, yet suddenly you came over and raised your hand as if to strike me. But you couldn't go through with it, instead summoning Eloy, who arrived with his slow gait and huge filthy feet; he picked me up like a sack of rubbish and threw me roughly down onto an armchair in the living room. He didn't smack me, or yell at me, he didn't even look at me; he simply raised his hand to his nose and blew loudly, hawking at the same time.

A viscous liquid coated his hand and he smeared it onto the chair next to my face, before disappearing.

I stood up and went to hide among the curtains. I sat there hugging my knees for a long time, until I was startled by the sound of footsteps. Like a procession, Noah, Mara, and Esther were advancing, carrying sheets and pillows. Trailing in their wake was my mother, in the arms of Felisberto and Eloy.

Still drowsy, she was dragging her feet. She wore only a petticoat and appeared hunched, her shoulder blades protruding.

Her jute-colored skin looked transparent and, from behind the curtain, I watched everything through particles of dust that had now turned into murky light.

And I did nothing to stop any of you, father, but deep down I thought: I see God, right now I can see God.

QUEEN OF THE ARTHROPODS

I hear the snorting of the horses, which grows ever louder. The shutters, previously closed, have been thrown open; they're there, muzzles pointing downwards, hanging their heads out of the window. From the door to my room I fling stones at their faces, but they continue to snort until they notice Felisberto and Eloy coming from the house. For the past two Thursdays, they've been leaving very early in the morning. They carry some produce, a few animals, and their figures are quickly swallowed by the mist.

Before leaving, Felisberto comes by my room; he opens the door, kicks the pile of saddles and orders me to prepare the ground for their return. I cast off the old blanket and get out of bed without bothering to cover my nakedness. He glares at me and turns to leave, coughing and hawking a great globule of phlegm onto my bed as he does.

"Clean this pigsty," he orders.

I nod and turn to fetch the broom. My backside is cold and my body shivers.

Father, I was always too weak. For everything. One night, you took me to see the newborn piglets. You picked up the smallest pig, the one that was dragging itself along among the others, as if blind, its legs twisted. Unable to so much as suckle, the rest jostled it aside with ease, and even did it harm. You grabbed it, moist as it was, and dumped it in a jute bag that you tied up and left to one side. My insides turned.

Even now that you're well and truly dead, father, you are still sometimes capable of unsettling my insides. Often, before acting, I find myself asking what you might say, what you would do. Nonsense, foolishness. There's nothing more worthless than the fears one grows accustomed to. You never liked the weak. You treated my mother in exactly the same way as you treated that piglet, removing her from your sight in order to avoid having to witness what you'd done to her.

Ultimately, father, that was very cowardly, worthy of a loudmouth who doesn't really understand his own actions. Like those children who use their slings to kill a bird, or any small animal, and then bolt, leaving the creature splayed on the ground because they can't bear to look at it. You weren't even a villainous villain. You were just an average man who got carried away on the little power you took from lording it over my mother and me, but no sooner did *they* arrive, big men with a tad more hair on their chests, than everything fell apart.

That night, what I'd wanted was to pick the piglet up, clutch it to my chest until I heard its final breath, and perhaps weep with it in my arms. I would even have buried it. But not now; if that happened now, I'd kill it with a single blow.

Felisberto and Eloy gallop off and the mist engulfs them. I walk over to our lands shrouded in cold. I pee beside the solitary elm, with my hand resting on its old, stripped trunk. Through the mist, I can see the elm is full of sparrows; some have lost feathers, others are missing a foot. For a few moments they appear completely motionless, until I observe them closing their eyes and moving their necks with those rapid tilts, as if this were their method of communicating, a kind of code I'm unable to decipher. When I remove my hand, they fly off and vanish just a few meters above me.

In the fields, I see the sun come out from behind our house, which resembles a nativity scene in the early morning light. The hoe marks the earth, but the wind erases its trail. This land is old, father, it no longer gives off warmth. The harvests are poor now; the fruit trees, though green, sometimes rot. And the corn husks sprout full of holes, yellow and deformed. The promised land bears no fruit. Only flesh can save us. But I fear flesh.

When I tilled Señor Elmur's land, he would make me tell him stories while he drank. I invented stories, distorting recollections and losing myself inside them, or I told him things I'd been taught by Professor Erlano. Once, I told him about the Battle of Waterloo, but ended up redeeming Napoleon and having him win, who knows why. Señor Elmur didn't even notice, my stories didn't matter to him, all he cared about was the voice, my voice. He listened without looking at me, as though my stories took him someplace else. He needed the sound and words to think about something I couldn't comprehend; he appeared to use my words to create something new and sordid.

My stories and the aguardiente must have relieved him of the cold, because, at the end of each workday, as I helped him back into the house, he would lean against my shoulder, passing the warmth from his armpits on to me, his face flushed, sweating as though with fever. Then he'd vomit everywhere and, before going to bed, I'd clean it up.

Is our land very cold now, father?

Allow me to tell you another story:

Kneeling at the foot of a steel-framed bed, a small boy imitated the sound of a cicada. In the steel-framed bed, a woman rested. Was the woman beautiful? In truth, she was no beauty to bewitch the little boy. She had a shrunken bosom and the ribs of a scrawny lamb. Her skin was cold and damp. What had the boy been given to touch that was similar?

The rotting roots of an unearthed plant.

The woman asked the boy again and again: "Who are you? And who gave you the gift of singing like the cicada?" I'm your son, the boy replied. And she would go quiet for several minutes, which to the boy were like entire rotations of the sun, and then tell him she had never had a child. Although, sometimes she told him she dreamed about a son who was part-boy, part-beetle, with a horn that stuck out imposingly from his head for fighting off men.

The woman spoke constantly of that dream child, saying: "With his boy legs he would run over to me, and I would wipe the blood from his horn with blankets which we burned in the middle of the garden in honor of our gods, our gods who have legs and wings, sometimes fur, sometimes claws."

It's me, your son, mother. The boy would repeat this in urgent whispers every time he went to see her, as she pulled out her hair, now nothing but fluff. She would yank it out and let the wind carry it away. There were parts of the woman's scalp that were nothing but raw flesh across which headlice roamed.

"Look at the dragonflies," said the woman, as she pulled out the hairs. "They fly far away." And the boy would catch them and try sticking them back to her head, but the hairs were no longer hers, and they flew, already transformed into dragonflies, winged.

The woman lived in captivity in a place with no wallflowers or chrysanthemums. The boy watched the white-clad ladies distrustfully, ice princesses, who tended her with veils pulled tightly around their equally hairless heads, now abandoned by the lice, because their hair, too, had turned into dragonflies. The woman didn't like that place, and the boy knew this and would have done anything for that woman, who never stopped asking: "Who are you, darling? It wasn't them who sent you, was it?" I'm your son, mamá, he repeated, and again she said she'd never had a son. That she had elms and a garden like the one belonging to her father and mother and grandfather and grandmother. But no son. No, no, no.

One day, the boy took a firm hold of her hand and said: "Mother, I'm your son. Look at me, mother, I have your eyes and hands, your slender fingers interrupted by a broad knuckle." She closed her eyes and touched his face with her clammy hands. "You're the boy who sings like the cicadas. Come, tell me. Who taught you how?"

I'm the count of the cicadas; they taught me. The boy said this to her as he concealed the shoots he carried in his hands, and again began to sing like the cicadas. Then he offered the shoots to the woman; she took them eagerly and, while putting them in her mouth, rocked her head to the rhythm of his song.

The woman began to laugh. She laughed incessantly as her eyes retreated. And even after she'd stopped breathing, she continued to laugh, saying: "I'm the Queen of the Arthropods."

THE HOUR OF THE ROSARY

One day, the Hour of the Rosary was held at our house. On that day, we were visited by all the town's genteel and horrid devotees, dressed in skirts reaching down to their ankles, blouses, and scarves tied around their necks in hues of ochre and clay. Pulled along by the arm were their husbands, plump lawyers I'd seen working inside tiny offices in town, surrounded by yellowing papers and smoking nonstop. They stirred up the dust as they approached along the path between the hills, as if arriving mounted on a cloud. Also in attendance were the Morattis, Father Hetz, and the Luppis, two brothers who'd become very wealthy, though no one quite knew how, and who always wore pastel-colored shirts with large stains on the sleeves.

You, father, had set out benches before an image of a painting of the Sacred Heart of Jesus. Once all were seated, it seemed Jesus looked down over them with the tenderest of gazes, his hair wavy and beard well groomed, as he pointed toward his bleeding heart ringed with thorns.

We prayed the Rosary, bead by bead, and also the Sorrowful Mysteries, as it was a Tuesday. And then we sang some litanies that spoke of Mary as the purest and most chaste of women, kind and full of grace. But it was all utterly absurd; no one in that place had a beard like Jesus, nor his blond hair, and none of those women were pure or kind or in any way graceful.

You were wearing a smile I'd never seen before, father. You were completely full of yourself, sitting with Felisberto and Eloy by your side. They were a head taller than you, and perched between them, sporting a ridiculous pompadour hairstyle and a too-tight necktie, you looked just like their ventriloquist dummy.

Once we'd finished, Esther knelt down and crossed herself in front of the painting. She and Noah began heading back and forth to the kitchen to bring out the food: chicken soup and aguardiente on silver platters. All imbibed their drinks with tiny sips. Things began to liven up when Eloy rose and went over to the piano, where he played some piercing melodies that could have withered the heart, but instead made everyone very happy, almost as much as the Sorrowful Mysteries; in particular, the Garden of Gethsemane and the Flagellation of that handsome Christ. The women, like a row of soldiers, arranged themselves to sit and eat their sandwiches on the large sofas. They sat very close together, their skirts modest and backs straight. When they spoke, they did so without making eye contact, murmuring things I didn't understand about fabrics and brocades and meringues and béchamel sauce. The men huddled in corners to talk about the rainy winter weather, sure to yield fat cobs of corn and plump turnips.

And all of this, all this fuss, had been organized so as to pray for my mother. But my mother never left her room. She'd turned into something in need of saving. You, father, wouldn't even visit her, only appearing at night to put the lock on that door, and then at lunchtime you would say things like "a spade's a spade" and "call things by their names," "God's plan is perfect" and "order and discipline instruct the soul." But you never went to see her, and now you'd gathered the entire town to save her, who knows what from.

My mother had spent days inside that room, father, taking something you all gave her that left her in a kind of limbo, her skin always clammy and very delicate. She was gaunt, all veins and tendons that, increasingly thick and protruding, formed a web beneath her skin that threatened to surface.

Her fine brown hair was always spread across the pillow, as though clinging to the bedsheets, sinking into them.

On the day of the Rosary, I just sat there on a stool in a pair of too-short cashmere pants, and a ridiculous white shirt that you'd ordered me to wear. When Noah and Mara called me to the kitchen to have dinner and go to bed, I obeyed without protest; however, taking advantage of the fact you were all distracted, I took the keys you'd left dangling from the pants you'd worn that morning and went to my mother's room to watch her sleep.

Her breathing was shallow, like a rabbit's kit, and her mouth hung open. The room was dark, and when I sat down in a corner to listen to her breathing, she woke.

"Fetch a candle and light the lamps, Lucas," she whispered.

I didn't say a word, I simply began to walk out of the room, heading cautiously to the courtyard, where I stole a candle; when I returned, my shadow preceded me down the dark corridor.

I lit the lamps one by one, and it wasn't until everything had become illuminated that I began to see the drawings on the walls. I thought of the cave paintings I'd once heard about from Professor Erlano when he came to give me classes, and in that moment could not recall their whereabouts; yet I knew they looked exactly like the ones inside my mother's room. The drawings were reddish and took the form of trees, thick trunks, roses, cockscombs, and alyssums. At the top, there was what looked like a rhinoceros or a beetle, and something else that may have been a spider, with legs so long they reached the ground, sheltering everything. Very fine lines delineated shamrocks and thicker lines created the deep-red grass.

And all of my mother's grass, animals, plants, and flowers were good. I imagined God weeding in his celestial garden, a wide-brimmed hat over his big, fat, invisible head, and becoming envious of my mother's garden, wielding his hoe with increasing violence, until everything was exactly as it had been before Genesis.

I drew nearer to her, wishing she were small enough for me to carry in my pocket and hide in my room, where I would have watched her for hours, but I could do no more than take hold of her hands. When I did so, I saw that her fingertips were swollen—I could almost feel them throbbing—and stained with flecks of blood, like tiny red lakes. Mamá didn't say a thing, she'd been relinquishing her words for many days, abandoning them as one might abandon one's gloves when it's no longer cold. But she allowed me to caress her fingers and began to close her eyes again.

I ran out to get water. One by one, I washed her fingers, using my shirt to clean and dry them; then I sat down beside her, very close, leaning my back against the bed, touching her incredibly fine hair and wiping her damp brow as I sang:

My mother is a rose
with faded petals
who keeps her scent
very close to her heart.
Enduring our sorrows
I'll never know how she cried
so when I speak of her ...

Mamá fell asleep and I knelt down to wipe the walls with my shirt, so no one but me would see them like that; yet red traces remained, as though a child had been playing with watercolors.

I walked along the dark corridor with a candle between my trembling hands. My shadows flickered like those of a damaged film reel, and with every step the sound of my feet became fainter against the long, silky notes of the piano that now rang out, louder and louder, through the house. When I went over to the living-room window, I saw that the women had left and only the pair of plump lawyers remained, their faces red and puffy, gulping down drinks and occasionally clinking glasses as they danced with Noah and Mara. My nursemaids' bosoms were pressed to those sweaty shirts, the men's hands at their waists, creasing the smock uniforms which were as stiff as ever. You were sitting in a chair, your tie loosened and your pompadour ruffled, and yet you smiled foolishly with the same eyes as that blond Jesus who allowed only his bleeding heart to be seen through the darkness.

From the kitchen came the sound of pots and pans, and when I went to look, I found Esther washing everything under a powerful jet of water, as she recited her infinite litany. "Get out of here. Go to bed, you naughty child," she said.

I felt like a stranger, wandering through the house but visible to no one, father. Heading to my room, I saw Sarai, running with her espadrilles half-off, her heels treading on the straps. She was leaving Felisberto's bedroom and making for the kitchen, her hair down and bouncing off her back. At that moment, the candle fell from my hands, breaking into large triangular pieces and other much smaller flat ones.

I thought how impossible it would be to pick that cursed candle up again. When Sarai turned and saw me, she said only: "Go to bed. This is no time for you to be up and about."

THE SPIDER

I adore Señorita Nancy. I discovered her wandering over by the untended shrubs and tired earth. She was observing a hole shaped like a volcano from which ants poured, hiding behind the trunk of an angel's trumpet, her velvety legs extended. What a joy it was to see her; in the dark of night, she was the purest black.

As soon as I noticed Señorita Nancy, I offered her my dirt-covered hand, but she didn't come to me. For days, I went looking for her in the same spot. I would watch her out of the corner of my eye, not talking, because spiders don't get tangled up in words. I did this again and again until finally she came over, timid at first, and perched at my feet. She moved her front legs as if wanting to carry on upwards, but uncertain, because spiders aren't as meddlesome as bees and wasps often are, always buzzing around you.

Spiders are born adult and elegantly dressed, their ostentatious legs and oval bodies recalling an attractive backside concealed behind a muslin gown.

My hand imitated her movements, though clumsily. Slowly, fingers extending joint by joint, I moved toward her, before flipping my hand, palm upwards, and inviting her to climb on. She didn't dawdle: she may be beautiful, but she isn't proud. She crawled along my fingers, caressing me with her eight velvety legs. I leaned back slowly and she came to rest on my naked torso. Suddenly, I felt a tiny nip and my chest stung. Which isn't bad, father. All the best things make your chest sting.

I've brought her back to my castle, for I've decided that's what it will be, a castle, but not the palace of a king. No, mine is the palace of a prince hidden among the weeds.

I put her down beside a flowerpot and she hasn't left, father. When I come back from working the land, I find her waiting for me by the door. I bring her dead flies and she gorges herself contentedly; I've occasionally eaten a few myself. I'll admit, they're an unusual meal with a flavor I'm unable to identify, but their texture is just like toasted breadcrumbs. Her greatest treats, however, are mice. I bring them back alive and wait to see her pounce on one and paralyze it; after she's eaten all they have inside, she piles them in a corner and returns to my bare chest, where she likes to sit and rest. She stretches out and lodges herself so firmly between my ribs, it's as if she has only just then emerged from my sternum.

In the mornings, I feed the pigs and horses. Afternoons, I till the earth, stack hay, harvest corn and onions. I drop everything at the door like an offering, and in exchange receive a stew tasting of leftovers that Sarai usually leaves for me in the stables at dawn, and which I don't normally eat because I'm a boy with common sense after all, and I feed off what I can scrounge for myself in the surrounding fields: water, berries, and a little fruit suffice.

On alternate days, I have to clean the water tank, and for now I'm as docile and obedient as a circus animal. Circus animals plan great catastrophes, which is why they're kept in separate cages. If all the world's circus animals were to band together, they'd kill us all for our sins.

At dawn, I climb the metal rungs and, before emptying the water tank, I dip my feet; first the soles, as they're the part that heats up most, and the water soothes them. Then, bit by bit, I slide in until I'm submerged in the water. I hold my breath, my cheeks inflate and my body begins to rise. Is there anything more beautiful than floating? If Felisberto and Eloy were to kill me, father, I would want them to leave my body in water until it wrinkled up; it would be almost like growing old, but at an unimaginable speed.

I come out of the water renewed. I scrub the sides of the tank as thoroughly as I can until my arms grow tired. When I finish, I gather in my hand a booty of three flies, a wasp, and a grub, all found by the edge of the water tank. Drowned and dead, but with their parts intact. I climb down carefully, using just one hand, because the other contains my gift for Señorita Nancy.

If Midas had invaded our house, I would have found it covered in gold leaf, but Felisberto and Eloy have touched it with their filthy hands. Everything here is putrid. The water tank will be kept clean, though, thanks to the prince, since Felisberto has acquired the habit of taking baths. Sprawled in the tub, he drinks aguardiente every night, not cleaning his parts, or washing his feet, or lathering himself with soap. He submerges his body in water and his throat in liquor. He doesn't clean himself, merely muddies the water. I've watched him on a number of successive evenings. Felisberto, with his head and feet sticking out of the tub, while Eloy plays frenetic melodies on the piano, like those you so enjoyed. The splashing and the music mix and Felisberto goes into a gruesome reverie. I'm becoming an excellent spy, father. I'm proud of myself, frankly. I evade my own presence and others cease to detect it. I've become empty of myself.

I am forbidden from entering the house, and if I do it's only to receive orders and, occasionally, beatings, because "This corn is soft and stinky!" Sarai, Mara, and Noah say nothing, remaining silent, loyal, and cruel. At least Esther would have sided with me, if only for a fight. I haven't thought of her in such a long time, it's as if she never existed. But this malodorous little thing, with no Esther or anybody, must bear the yelling and humiliations and bow his head, father, and issue curses only on the inside, toward his innards, swelling up with millions of sons of bitches and giant shit bags, dirty sneaks and vultures, dimwits and dickheads.

Señorita Nancy agrees that this is no way to talk to a prince, and sometimes I come across her seeming meditative, legs extended, hairs standing on end, thinking of ways to get inside and give everyone a good going-over, because spiders and scorpions have a duty to punish wickedness. After eating what I've brought her, Señorita Nancy goes about her business. With that delicate way she has of weaving her web, she teaches me to trace geometric shapes. I watch her, and she shows off her knowledge of logic and mathematics. My mother and Professor Erlano would have been devoted to her too. They would have been moved by seeing her weave perfect radii, tirelessly, one after another, until achieving a spectacle of concentric triangles, finally connecting these with ever-smaller circles. When she finishes her spiderweb, she perches in the center to rest and patiently await the coming of her prey. Everything has its time, father. And everything we desire, under the sky or in a spiderweb, has its moment.

Before heading into the fields, I make a lap around the house, dragging myself along the ground and spying on all I can. Noah and Mara are darning socks, buried in the sofa, with faces like corpses; they darn huge socks, like brown-colored sacks, filthy in spite of being washed. Then, without meaning to, I allow my presence to be detected, and they turn to look at me. I begin to snarl and run, but I see that Felisberto is coming after me.

"Come here," he yells.

I look at him; his chest is bare and his lump-covered bones gleam in the first rays of sunlight. His skeleton could pass for an attraction at Señor Lazlo's fair: people would line up to see it.

I turn and run, not hesitating. Though he

shouts again, I continue to run across the dead earth.

"By Sunday, Elmur will have come for you, you little bastard," he yells more loudly.

When I turn to look, he's no longer there. Only the house, dark and still.

PROFESSOR ERLANO'S NOSE

It was Professor Erlano's fleshy nose that indicated to me the things worth learning about the world. A nose that preceded him. Big and bulging. On the septum, there were small, skin-colored pimples I would swear changed places when a person closed their eyes. And it had yet another extraordinary feature: the nostrils never opened; that whole nose was incredibly still, like a stout homunculus that would perspire whenever Professor Erlano attained the highest levels of excitement, with even his rectangular lenses beginning to fog up. When something truly moved him, the large pores on his nose would open, discharging tiny droplets that made it glisten. He might be speaking about the fantastic ugliness of Polyphemus, or Napoleon riding with feet barely touching the stirrups in the midst of the Battle of Austerlitz, but inside my mind everything would be acquiring that sheen of exaltation. The history of the world reached me through that thick nose, an organ appearing to have a will and identity all of its own.

Everything else about Professor Erlano was perfectly plain and simple. He was a thin man with hardly any hair and just a single blue suit. His jacket may well have been attached to his shirt, and when it was hot, he simply rolled up the sleeves.

The last time I saw Professor Erlano, his blue pants were wrinkled, and I remember Esther saying, "Dear God, I'll iron them myself if you like." While heading up to the sitting room, he made a vain attempt at smoothing them out, Esther following behind and staring intently as I squeezed her forearm in the hope of keeping her quiet. But she was incorrigible. On every stair, she repeated, "Enough, child, let go of my arm."

For our lessons, we always went to the second-floor sitting room, settling down across from each other at a little table upon which Professor Erlano opened up his briefcase and took out books on history, mythology, mathematics, and botany, and we would set about studying these simultaneously, the gods of Olympus walking over trapeziums before leaping toward the highest branches of the *Eucalyptus L'Hér* that populated the Andean highlands. My mother used to sit behind us on a sofa and listen attentively to the lessons, her legs crossed beneath a black notebook where she jotted down unconnected words: polytopes, theodolite, Heliogabalus, despots. Later, she would call trees, plants, and shamrocks by these names.

Ever since my mother had been sent to the back room, I took my classes alone and from time to time the professor or I would turn to glance over at the sofa—sometimes me, sometimes him—to confirm she really wasn't there. Whenever Professor Erlano finished discoursing on some topic, he would slide his glasses down and, in a quiet voice, ask if my mother was feeling any better. I never knew how to respond, and he would slide his glasses back up and sit there, apparently lost in thought, or perhaps in something resembling melancholia. The day of my final lesson, he was talking to me about Napoleon, and flew into a rage on imagining the Little Corporal riding with his heels free from their stirrups: "Le Petit Caporal, bâtard!" he exclaimed. And that nose glistened as Austerlitz fell to the French, and I imagined a tiny little fellow with a voice like the men on the radio screaming at his soldiers, all taller than him. Professor Erlano cried out in imitation of the battle, becoming more and more worked up, and although I didn't understand, I pretended to raise a sword so as not to dampen his enthusiasm.

"In fact," you said, father, having come up to join us in the sitting room at that moment, leaning against the doorframe, "Napoleon's actual height was 1.68 m, almost five foot six and a half inches from his head to his heels, much larger than the average citizen of the time, *Señor* Erlano." The professor stood up immediately and extended his hand to you. But you, father, so full of your own self-importance, limited yourself to a curt nod, leading the proffered hand to make a final vain attempt at smoothing out the pants.

Then I recall how you began explaining

that Napoleon had appeared so much smaller because he was always on the battlefield alongside his best soldiers, who were all very tall and stocky. Who knows where you'd acquired so much information about all this; the truth is, I'd never heard you speak about history, or anything else for that matter. Come to think of it, apart from those ready-made phrases you uttered when we sat down to table, I'd be hard-pressed to say what exactly it was you did talk about.

What was it you loved most, father? What were you afraid of as a child? Were you ever a child? Who were you?

It was at this exact moment that I was able to see you clearly: to me, you were Napoleon. Your voice was strange and spoke in a language I could not understand. Around us, your stature was normal, but between Felisberto and Eloy you were a min-

iscule creature. By their side you were waging your great war, a sinister expansion plan. They were your tall and stocky soldiers. That day, you won another of your

129

disgusting battles: you told Professor Erlano you'd decided to dispense with his services, that there had been plenty of discussion, and it was felt that the best thing for me would be to begin boarding at the Jesuits' college from the start of the new term.

I knew if I tried to say anything, you'd summon them. You'd summon Felisberto or Eloy to immediately remove me from your sight, before saying the Our Father at table and offering thanks for your family. There was nothing I could do but watch as the lean and kindly Professor Erlano, with his majestic nose, left the house with the entire world inside his briefcase.

Sitting on the porch, I watched him grow ever smaller.

When I was about to go back inside, Professor Erlano turned and hurried over, placing the briefcase on his knees and taking from it a book we'd never looked at before in class. It was bound in coffee-colored leather, peeling like damp trees. It was smooth and heavy, and smelled of all things far away and exotic. I opened the book at a random page, like someone prone to superstition:

It can sometimes take years to witness a complete metamorphosis. Some insects won't emerge from their pupa for a very long time.

"It's for you and your mother," he told me.

He glanced in both directions and then left, moving very quickly this time, hand still smoothing his pants, until he disappeared.

It was that night, with the book in my hands and my body feverish, that I made up my mind to leave that house. I would get my mother out of there, and together we'd go someplace we could create an enormous garden full of melody and life. That was the first time, father, that I decided you ought to disappear from our lives. In the darkness, I clenched my teeth and a dark tingling began to invade my body. A person can live without a father, I told myself, but never in the same house as Napoleon.

I don't believe I contemplated your dying, or perhaps I did, but I remember imagining you dead already. One day you existed, and the next, just by crossing my fingers, you were gone.

The mind of a child doesn't solve problems, doesn't contemplate overcoming obstacles; it simply thinks what it would be like to win.

THE CICADAS

The hay is cold and the grass I carry wet. It's raining in that tiresome way it does up in the hills, with fat droplets that seem to explode upon landing. Felisberto and Eloy's horses are not here. I lie down in the hay, which is as fragrant as ever, and leave the grass by my feet so I can sink them into it. If it weren't for those devilish horses, this could be a place for me to hide.

On the other side of the wooden divider, I watch as someone cleans their feet in a large clay bowl, the bowl the horses drink from. The feet appear to be covered in dirt. I creep over, and from under the wooden partition grab an ankle. I feel the jolt. I stick my head out through the gap. It's Sarai, and she looks down, before beginning to pull me through the gap between the partition and the ground as if I were a cat, grasping me by the underarms and setting me down in front of her.

As soon as my feet touch the ground, I push her with both hands, a forceful shove to the navel. She grabs me tightly by the wrists and I tense up. I resist and kick out violently, we struggle until one of her feet steps back onto the edge of the bowl and smashes it, and from that foot blood begins to seep like paint that spreads and colors everything a dirty red. She holds me to her chest and I no longer resist. The blood mixes with the earth and water. We're an island. She says I'm hers. "You're my Lucas. My love." I rub my eyes, squeezing my wrists in between her stomach and my face. I begin to disentangle myself, but slowly, accepting her presence. I look her up and down. She has her hair tied up in a high bun, her cheekbones more prominent than ever; hers is a skull-like beauty, elegant, hard, unbreakable.

I look at her mistrustfully, because that's what she would always say on seeing me when I was a child. "Come here, my love," she would say, back when I was little and could belong to whoever it was that loved me, before I became the thing I am now. A body empty of myself, filled with rancorous silence.

Sarai's brow is sweaty and her greasy hair gathers in fine threads that fall and stick to her back and neck. Slowly, she kneels at my feet and says over and over how sorry she is for having let them throw me out of my own home. She rests her hands on my chest and begins to cry as though she were a little girl. With hiccupping. I count the hiccups—ten —and the seconds between them—five. Stop crying, be a good girl, I want to tell her. But now she speaks again and muddles up my counting. How horrific life is inside that house! I can't imagine the things they make them do. Sins that nobody, in any place, should ever hear of. Nothing can redeem her, she's sure of that, but she wants me to go far away. *Don't come back, for the love of God.*

I do not love God. God has absolved me from loving him.

She says she'll help me, that she has money and knows someone in town.

I care for her; I confess it. For a second, I

care deeply for her because she is filled with guilt. I put my hands around her neck, kneel before her, and bury my head in her bosom and feel her breasts and become an idiot, a complete idiot, hypnotized by the animal scent that emanates from beneath the sheer fabric of her petticoat. This isn't a betrayal; at the first glimmer of love, an abandoned dog or cat would go to pieces over any good-for-nothing.

I feel as if my other self were watching this scene. I feel my chest swell, trembling and stinging, as though Señorita Nancy were perched atop it. Then I look upon the frozen scene, the tableau pressing down on my heart. This is not my true nature. I'm simply tired, and it's easier to settle than to be just. I would rest upon her bosom forever if I were weaker.

Sarai pulls away and touches my face as if wiping away tears, tears that aren't there. I gaze at her unblinkingly, but this is not a game. The chicken hand slides down my chest and rests upon my sex, half covering it. I experience a sudden shudder, an urge to bring my legs together and squeeze them tightly, as though I were peeing. She just looks at me, enveloping me with those large eyes that crown her cheekbones. My body throbs; I worry that she feels it, that she can feel it through my skin, through the worn fabric. The throbbing of my shame. I look at her hand, the gently caressing fingers; the skin around her nails has tiny flakes that curl up like sawdust, falling downwards and filling her hand. Perhaps her body is covered in that rotting flesh.

Sarai's hand, which was supposed to one day give rise to a newborn child's hand that I would watch grow for years, is now rehearsing for its transformation into a decrepit hand. That hand has already touched dead and corrupted skin. I remove it quickly, stand up, and begin to snarl as I edge backwards. I snarl and clench my fists. I move toward the doorway, leaving her kneeling, weeping to herself; she doesn't come after me, nor do I hope she will. I cast a final empty look at her, with the eyes of a dead cat.

It's now, when I know I almost strayed from the path, father, when I came very close to stumbling, that I'm able to accept the vision that pursues me. My wrath is unlike that of God, who hurts where he loves; my wrath is cold and calculating.

If we were to measure the antennae of any insect, we would see they leave no room for imperfection. Millimeter by millimeter, their parts always match, pair by pair; identical. Wings, legs, antennae. The sancta sanctorum of symmetry. Everything about them is calculated and pure and divine. When people see horror in them, when you, father, used to look at them with repulsion, you were seeing only yourself. Flies provoke rejection and repugnance because they remind us of what will come when our bodies transform into something rotten. The still-intact shell of a beetle can demonstrate nothing but eternity and beauty. God is formless and, as such, an idiot.

The squishy white larva turns into a fly, the pupa into a beetle. I leave the stables and run under the cold rain. I run to my mother's garden. I run as if I were racing toward a living forest, because for the first time I know what I have come here to do, father. I see it clearly. I kneel and scrabble with my nails, wanting only to lie back and surround myself with earth. I dig a pit that quickly becomes a tunnel, my dark damp tunnel, where I can hear the sound of the insects that surround me, hear the cicadas so near at hand. Trumpets and choirs.

When the angel of hell discovered he'd been exiled, he created a kingdom more powerful than that above. I will create a kingdom too, father. I'm listening to it. I will raise my church above this kingdom, I will have an altar crowned with butterflies and larvae; I'll forever kiss the beetles, pray before all spiders, and march with scorpions, for this house belongs to them.

Lying back in my temple, I join in with the singing of the cicada. The song of annunciation.

THE ANNUNCIATION

It was February, carnival month. Everywhere there was a lethargy, a sultriness that warned of a downpour. The warm, hazy air rose up during the nights making it impossible to sleep. For days now the clouds had been coming and going, returning darker and denser each time but never quite committing to rain.

Dried-out tadpoles could be seen stuck to the edges of ponds, covered in mud, their tails shimmering in the sun. The earth was cracked; the yellow ears of corn looked tired; bougainvillea shed their dry petals, leaving their stalks naked and violent; and pigeons dropped from their rooftop nests, dying of pure thirst.

But still the rain did not come.

Felisberto and Eloy would don their black

clothing and head out each day to till the soil, their equally black kerchiefs wrapped around their heads. And yet, our lands appeared dead, ruined by a harsh light; dry, and liable to burst into flame at the spark of a match. Felisberto asked for patience, father. He spoke to you of a great downpour, of parched fields that would then become green again. In other times, your word, father, would have prevailed, you would have taken charge of your own lands and your home and thrown them out, but your own word no longer existed and you granted them patience, afforded them all the time in the world. You allowed them to stay and deliver on their promise to you.

When Felisberto and Eloy returned from the fields, Sarai would already have everything laid out on the table for them. She even seemed happy to give them exactly what they wanted, which was nearly always venison and quail. Sarai had learned to prepare every dish that could be made with quail: baked quail, fried quail, medium-rare, quail with mushrooms, quail in apple sauce, quail eggs with corn, quail eggs on bread.

I would hide. I'd flee from everyone and make for the rocky cave behind the *Polylepis* forest. The cave was hidden behind a wall of thickets, concealing it from all but those who already knew of its existence. It was cool and dry, and I'd begun building an apachita in the entrance: a pyramid of stones that grew like an offering to the mountain whenever I crossed it. Inside, it was dark, a cold stone shelter, like the mountain's womb. If you kept very still and quiet, you could see how spiders and scorpions filed out of the cracks. Inside the cave, I learned to become a hard stone statue, to stand watch for hours. I played a solemn and exacting game with those insects, aware that they were more powerful than I was. One false move and they'd disappear, like the gods of a temple that could only be summoned by becoming empty of one's self.

I would spend nearly all day in the cave. I read and carefully examined the Book, the one left to me by Professor Erlano. I'd torn out the first page, an illustration of an old and strikingly beautiful woman, and affixed it to one of the cave walls. The woman was depicted surrounded by butterflies, flowers, and grubs, by pages covered in drawings of insects.

The image seemed to look directly into one's eyes, as if gazing out of another world; an old world, yellow and diaphanous like the paper it was made of.

Sometimes, I'd find myself dazzled by her image. She shone in the darkness of my cave, with that black bonnet covering her head, those prominent cheekbones, that almost cadaverous face. Only her eyes seemed youthful: she had the surly gaze of a little girl. One day, Esther discovered me inside the lair, kneeling before the image of that woman. She walloped me then: "God will lay your lifeless body before the lifeless bodies of your idols," she told me.

She fought her way out of there, pulling me after her by the arm and scratching both our knees in the process. And she frightened the insects, those dark gods of my temple, until a spider, small but beautiful, bit her on the calf. Esther rubbed the bite repeatedly as her brow and nose began to sweat and she scolded me for behaving like such a ruffian.

I managed to wriggle free of her vicelike grip and run back to the house, waving my arms in the air and roaring with laughter, thinking how one day God would allow my lifeless body to lie before the body of that woman in the image.

Esther's heavy frame followed behind me; disgruntled, she told Sarai and Noah that she would not be putting up with any more nonsense. Sarai prepared some vinegar and baking soda for the bite and as she applied the ointment, Esther told them: "Somebody needs to take charge of Lucas." What she said didn't displease me. After all, she was the only one who still came looking for me when I hid. Sometimes she would even bathe me, though I'll admit that the force with which she scrubbed my back, armpits, and crotch would increase with every hoarse, tired sermon she launched into. But I liked that she took charge of me and, what's more, I never listened.

I only had eyes and ears for the Book. Not even the Book of the Generations of Adam was as perfect as the one I'd been given. A universe greater than any I'd previously imagined was opening up before me with its symmetrical, subterranean lifeforms. It was full of illustrations and life, of new words and names, just like my mother's books. And the words in that Book rang so loudly in my ears that I failed to notice the signs of what was approaching: the sultriness that increased each night as we sat down to table with those men, and the heat that filled the space so completely. And you, father, wiping the sweat from your brow with trembling hands, always agitated. And that burning sensation that prickled all over our bodies, leaving us in a state of lethargy to which Felisberto and Eloy appeared somehow immune.

"It seems it will finally rain tonight!" you would repeat every evening while the table was cleared, mopping the sweat from your brow as though something were asphyxiating you. But no one responded.

It was on the final day of that month, with Uncle Eugenio's arrival at the house, that the heavens opened, culminating in a hailstorm that covered everything in a slippery white blanket. And yet, before the night was through, it had all melted to leave a pool of dirty water around our house.

MADHOUSE

Uncle Eugenio had come to visit with his two daughters, twins Esther described as looking like a pair of dolled-up mice: Teresa and Alba. During dinner, the billowing sleeves of their dresses hovered just above their plates, dipping into the broths and sauces as they chewed the food noisily with their sharp little teeth.

My uncle would bring his fists back down onto the table after every mouthful, his knife and fork clenched tightly in each hand. He ate quickly, swallowing large pieces of half-chewed meat and taking big gulps of his wine. At first sight, nobody would have said that Uncle Eugenio was your brother, father. His head was entirely bald, but on his face he sported thin sideburns that sprouted at his temples and gave way to a bushy white beard.

All of the wrinkles on Uncle Eugenio's face seemed to stem from his eyes, the circular creases spreading upwards, across his cheeks, and down around his mouth. It was these wrinkles that made him appear harmless, and somehow also less fat than he actually was.

The twins could not stop fidgeting throughout the entire meal, but Uncle Eugenio barely glanced at them. When Esther shot a reproving look their way, Teresa rose and said: "Good Señora, do you always just sit there watching how everybody eats?"

As soon as they'd finished their meal, the twins dragged me upstairs to the sitting room, because they wanted to see the house. At the top of the stairs, Teresa wiped her hands on her skirt.

"This house is like a damned relic," she said. "Does nobody water the ferns?!" she added, as she ran the tips of her fingers over each of the plants that hung from the wall.

Alba agreed with everything her sister said. "That's what it looks like, yes. Nobody, nobody waters them."

"Our father says your mamá's nerves have

given out, Lucas. The same thing happened to one of our mother's aunts," Teresa began telling me, as she sat with her legs crossed and rested her head against the large leg of an armchair.

"Lots of people went to visit her but no one could make head nor tail of what the poor woman said to them. She said she could see things from the future, long lines of people who wandered aimlessly, because in the future no one had a home. The cities were like great walled houses, which only a select few could enter. They said she spoke of things like that, things people see when they're cuckoo. They found her one day consulting with a curandera. Apparently they were both cackling incessantly. That's what my mother said, that it frightened her, seeing them both laughing with their mouths open so wide, like madwomen, with no sense of decorum."

"Yes, exactly. Mamá said they were laughing uncontrollably. People who laugh like that frighten her, they really, really frighten her. When we laugh, she tells us to restrain ourselves, to laugh without showing our gums," said Alba.

"We wanted to see your mother. Because of the laughter thing. We'd like to see someone laugh like that," Teresa added, coming toward me as she adjusted her hairband, which had slipped down over her eyes.

"Is it true? My father says that's why we came. To help your father sort things out. He says there are places for people like your mamá, not in this town, but in ours. But we wanted to see her before it all gets settled. Have you ever seen her laugh like that?"

Teresa never stopped talking, and Alba just continued agreeing with everything she said. I felt dizzy.

"On closer inspection, Lucas, you look quite terrible yourself. Look at your hair, you're like a little savage."

At that moment, Teresa reached her hand toward my head, wanting to touch my hair to demonstrate her point. I grabbed her hand firmly to prevent her and we stared straight into each other's eyes, until, embarrassed, I released her and ran off. She had eyes like the woman in my cave. The eyes of a little animal-girl.

The twins pursued me all over the house.

"Little savage boy?" Teresa called out. "Come back here!"

And Alba was like a parrot trailing after her, repeating: "Savage and stupid. Savage and stupid."

You, Uncle Eugenio, Felisberto, and Eloy were still in the dining room, so I made for my nursemaids' room to hide.

There I found Esther, Noah, and Mara almost asleep. Only Sarai's bed was empty. I hid behind the door and watched through the cracks as Teresa and Alba searched for me. And then I saw them go into Felisberto's room.

I had never been in Felisberto's room. I'd imagined it a thousand times; in my mind it was full of mud and rats. And it smelled foul.

I went after them and grabbed Teresa by the skirt.

"You can't go in there. It's *their* room," I told her.

"No one told me not to, cowardly little savage boy."

"Cowardly, savage, and stupid," echoed Alba.

The three of us went in. None of what I'd

imagined was true. There was nothing out of the ordinary about the room. The bed and furniture were the same as before they'd arrived, and there were dozens of those black outfits they always wore, the same black shirts and cloaks hanging again and again inside the wardrobes on wooden hangers, also painted black. In the darkness, they resembled thousands of men like Felisberto, but without their heads.

"How boring," said Teresa. "Once, in our cook Carmela's room, we found photographs of her naked from the waist up. Next to the photographs there were letters from a Jorge Juan Gómez Pérez. Now, Señor Gómez Pérez *was* interesting, and said things like: 'Punish me to your heart's content, my sweet and dirty little bird.' Now that was amusing. Wasn't it, Alba?"

"Alba?" She called out again, because her echo seemed to have disappeared.

We turned our heads and saw Alba on the other side of the room, holding a wooden box in her hands.

"Alba?"

We went over to her and looked inside the

box. It held a stash of cylindrical keys, many very old, some rusty, others new and very small, but all like rotten bones reeking of decay. We removed them one by one; they were cold and worn.

At the bottom of the box, there was a black-and-white drawing. We held it up to the oil lamp in the corner to get a better look. It was a drawing of a small huddle of men, and on their faces it was just possible to make out some hastily sketched features that made them appear deranged; some were dressed in black rags, while others were completely naked or wearing gowns that revealed their backsides.

At the edge of the drawing, in smudged, handwritten letters was scrawled the word: *Madhouse.*

Teresa and I stared straight into each other's eyes again. We breathed almost in sync, as again and again Alba repeated: "Madhouse, madhouse, madhouse."

"Quiet now, Alba María de los Dolores!" Teresa told her.

We hurried out of the room. We were crossing the courtyard to get to my bedroom when fat droplets began to fall from the sky, and before we could reach the other side, these had turned into a fierce downpour, with hail that pounded the ground and bounced violently in all directions.

THE EXPULSION

The three of us huddled at the foot of my bed as the rain and hail began to fill everything with noise. Teresa removed her socks and instructed Alba and me to do the same; Teresa's nose whistled and Alba began scratching at the wooden floor as she frantically jiggled her right knee, her leg brushing against Teresa's and causing me to tremble as well.

There was a cry from Uncle Eugenio, so we went outside. We couldn't hear what was being said, but from time to time someone would slam his fist down on the table.

"You're a bloody fool," said Uncle Eugenio, once the rain had begun to ease.

"He said *bloody*," whispered Alba.

Teresa wasn't looking at Alba; she only had eyes for me. We began to walk along the corridor, circling the courtyard until we reached the door to the kitchen and tucked ourselves behind some jute sacks smelling of potato peels and weeds. Esther came into the kitchen and strained some coffee, before sitting down to drink it from an unwashed beer glass.

"Have you even seen your wife?" said Uncle Eugenio. "Who bathes her? How long since you last visited her? Why won't you let them clean her, you animal?"

"Don't come here and tell me how to treat my own wife."

"I won't take this problem off your hands," said Uncle Eugenio. "Your house is like a brothel. A dirty brothel!"

At that moment, Felisberto appeared in the corridor that led to the kitchen, with my mother in his arms. She was so weak she could only moan. He set her down in the middle of the kitchen and threw a bucket of water over her.

Esther rose from the table and ran over to my mother, yelling for Felisberto to stop. "This is ungodly, Don Miguel."

Felisberto shoved her and Esther hit her hip against the table. Then she knelt down, still rubbing her right side, and began to pray.

My uncle came over and tried to stop Felisberto, but you, father, told him to keep out of it.

"Didn't you want her cleaned?" you yelled.

"Have you gone mad, Miguel?" said Uncle Eugenio, taking a step back.

"Under my roof, we do as I command," was the last thing you said.

And you did not command him to, but at that moment Uncle Eugenio, with his wrinkled face that made him appear less fat than he actually was, marched out of the kitchen and stumbled over one of the sacks the three of us were hiding behind. He looked at the twins as if about to scold them, but didn't; he simply picked them up off the ground and carried them away, one under each arm. Their hair was dishevelled, they were sockless, and their bare feet bounced up off the ground as Uncle Eugenio carried them out of the house and into the hailstorm.

I came out from behind the sacks and ran over to my mother. Wrapping my arms around her bowed neck, I tried to avoid the vertigo of meeting her eyes.

Esther put her arms around me and called

out for Sarai to take me away, but Sarai didn't come. You, father, lifted me roughly by the arm and threw me into a corner. Then you delivered a heavy blow to Esther, who was still kneeling to my mother's right. She rose and looked directly at you, her breathing heavy, then turned away, muttering only: "May God forgive you. I cannot."

In the distance I could see Sarai, Noah, and Mara, who were watching everything from the door to their room. As soon as they noticed me, the door shut.

Esther ran outside, espadrilles flapping against her heels as they grew soaked under the hail. She went to talk to Uncle Eugenio as he saddled up the horses. Esther wanted to help the twins up into the carriage. Alba climbed in, timid and docile, but Teresa began to shake her head and wriggle, tugging at her father's arm and pointing toward me: "Bring Lucas," she cried.

Uncle Eugenio didn't answer her. Who was going to agree to take me away from there? I was in my own home, after all, with my father and mother. Once Uncle Eugenio had everything ready, he picked up Teresa and put her inside the carriage, her bare feet kicking the air. The last person to climb in was Esther.

THE MOUNTAIN INSECTS

It was a slender cane you used during the final days of your life. No one knew why, but I always suspected. You were already condemned. You'd been hobbling around the house, and then one day you appeared with that cane. I liked it because the pale, cedar-like wood resembled Señor Lazlo's wooden leg, with its meticulously carved ants frozen in time.

Though not adorned with any carvings, the cane's handle boasted a puma made of shells and pearl. On you, the puma would rest between the index and middle fingers, seeming to spring forward as you walked. You used that cane to go everywhere; when you stood still, your two hands would fall over the puma, covering it completely, and when you went to bed, I'd watch you place it under your pillow and grip it tightly with one hand. I could smell your fear from a distance, and couldn't help suspecting that part of the reason you kept it was to wield it as a weapon.

What use would that cane have been to you! Nothing but a prop for your dying body.

When I returned to this house, I saw the cane, damp and covered in leaves, standing in a corner as if you still gripped it with both hands. What rests upon the cane now is the rigid body left by Señorita Nancy after her most recent transformation: black and shiny, like polished patent leather, with velvet trimmings on the legs. So hard and compact, it's difficult to believe she could have removed it in the way she did: turning upside down and, with microscopic movements of her legs, beginning to slip out of herself like a true contortionist.

The day draws near, father. I should hurry. Before Sunday, I will have left. Your cane is now our staff of command, our emblem. The eternal form.

When the sun goes into hiding, I head for the chamber pot and sit for several minutes, meditating in that scent of urine. Now I can see everything clearly, a plan bubbling away like broth amid the ammonia vapors. Tomorrow will be the day. Here, we have the house, the barbarians, and the cyclopes of this old and corrupted world.

I grip the cane tightly, for it will guide my steps. Señorita Nancy is coming with me, and I tread with the lightness of a shadow. I'm afraid, and that spurs me on. I cross my mother's garden as I did when I was very little and would cross dark corridors, screaming on the inside. I swell up with fear. It's what hurries me onward, on the tips of my toes, keeping me at an altitude of a thousand meters, as if above the clouds, with a bitter taste in my mouth.

With the cane in my hand, I step out of my castle as soon as it grows dark. I leave everything behind and begin to climb the hill directly opposite this house. It has a slope that protrudes like a gigantic, perfectly straight nose; in town they call it the Devil's Nose. I follow the path that leads up the hill, a small goat trail that serves as a shortcut. Everything else is covered in scree and moss.

The path grows steeper as I advance. We scale a set of unmoving features made of earth, rock, and tussock grass. The cane helps me climb steadily.

As I proceed, I close my eyes and touch everything, for the mist is but a single dense mass, like water. Within it, our lungs become useless and hinder us; within the mist, it is our eyes that are confused. With eyes closed and hands extended, it's easier to feel the mist's thick, heavy texture.

The mist disperses as I part it with my arms, but in the manner it always does, slow and indifferent. I've learned to swim in it. I don't allow it to disconcert me because I look inward, where it cannot reach. The mist is a shield around the forest, giving way only when it wishes us to enter. As I climb, the vegetation becomes hostile, the nettles sting my legs and the smell of rue assaults my nose as the tussock grasses crowd ever closer, until a path surrounded by paramo shrubs opens up before me.

The trail continues to fold back on itself, and behind me I can hear the chatter of the paramo, the wind that's slipped its chains, the whispering of thousands of branches.

By the time the mist recedes completely, I've reached the top. It's the mountain that has allowed us to arrive. Way up here, the vegetation becomes more rugged, the plants more densely packed, encircling the rocks. Everything is damp, cold, and tangled; the condensed air of the paramo coalesces and distills life. Where one least expects, there are rivulets of water so crystalline one can't avoid sinking one's feet into them. I press down firmly on the tussock grass, one hand over the other, and from beneath I feel water seep from the ground's very pores. I collect some in my hands to wash the sweat from my brow and quench my thirst.

The mountaintop is as boundless as another sky.

From here I should be able to see our house, but there's no light, only mist. I plunge my cane into the carpet of vegetation that covers everything and fall to my knees, my cheeks stinging from the burning cold. But I get back up and walk, it's only a little further until I reach the *Polylepis* forest and, from there, the cave. I don't think that you, father, ever reached the forest; your practical, subservient eyes would have been no use to you in a place like this. Perhaps you would have seen nothing, bar a load of twisted trees or a good place for gathering wood.

My mother brought me here only once. The *Polylepis* forest is the furthest I have ever ventured. How far did you travel, father? Did you ever leave the ruins of your own head?

Behind the *Polylepis* forest, the sun dies. We're high up, so high the trees appear to bow to avoid touching the clouds. The *Polylepis* are paramo trees. Their trunks peel and drop clusters of soft, living leaves. The wind reaching them is so strong they are contorted, twisted, deformed by gales, stretching now to one side, now the other; their trunks snake almost parallel to the ground.

I pass between the stooped trunks, and for a moment they give me vertigo. I pick up small stones and damp *Polylepis* leaves. When I reach the cave, Señorita Nancy overtakes me and enters first.

I leave the stones on the apachita. Rites, father, are important to mountains.

I enter the cold gloom of my sacred grotto,

remaining silent with my eyes wide open so they can grow accustomed to the darkness. I touch the stone walls until I feel them: scraps of the pages from the Book are still here. She is looking at me, I'm certain of it. I search around the edges, under rocks covered in moss. Here lies the Book, damp and cold as a lizard. I place it on the floor of the cave and lean back inside my temple. I inhale as deeply as I can, to relax my breathing, quickened by the climb. Little by little, I become a statue, a statue with a cane in its hand. Señorita Nancy crawls along the cracks; I watch her inch forward and then close my eyes for a long while. Suddenly, I hear an echo that begins to expand.

This is the endgame, father.

Señorita Nancy approaches. But she's not alone. Behind her I can hear more legs scuttling across the stones. Señorita Nancy crawls up onto my chest and they follow, they scale my feet, spread over my body and walk. This is my desire, and it pulses and climbs and rattles. Some cling to the fine hairs on my legs and crawl up. I feel the timidity of their touch, their tiny legs that dig into my pores, protecting me.

My chest stings, father, but I let them do it. They are the keepers of this temple, and now they are inside me.

PUPA

Before dawn, I begin my descent. With me I bring Señorita Nancy, some spiders, scorpions, and damselflies. They can't harm me now, father. They're my guardians, clad in their gleaming black armor, that outer skeleton, that non-living matter that offers them such protection. I also bring clumps of nettles, rue, poppies, Andean daisies, gaultheria, oleander, and chocho roots. My mother never came down from the mountain without buds, shoots, and leaves that she would leave in water for days until they put out roots. Later, she transplanted them to the garden, wandering around with those shrubs in her hands as if they were extensions of her body. Sometimes I believed that when my mother undressed and sank into a bath run by Esther, it was to moisten tiny roots sprouting from her armpits and groin.

But I was no root, no leaf, no stalk, and my mother knew this. Between my mother and me, there had always been an imaginary distance like that which exists between the identical poles of two magnets, that invisible force more immovable than any block of stone, because you cannot topple a magnetic field. Sometimes, I believed this distance was marked out in your name, father. That my mother could smell how, within me, I harbored your thick, foul-scented blood. Through your fault, through your fault, through your most grievous fault. My mother would have been happier had a succulent emerged from her womb. Even a dull, curly-leafed legume would have been preferable, one that smelled of earth and water rather than flesh and blood.

But now I'm closer to her, father.

Once I finish my herbalist's walk, I take my plants and guardians back to the castle, where I rest and read the Book until the sun comes out completely.

In the beginning, father, it was believed that insects originated from evil, from stench and putrefaction. All insects were supposed to be held in abomination. As if the world had made itself, born of two spirits: one good, one evil. The woman I had been worshipping when Esther surprised me had looked at the world with her sacred eyes and created it anew. She observed how that miniscule world was taking shape in silence. And, unnoticed, it has left its descendants everywhere, membrane upon membrane, thousands of eggs pulsing in unison, larvae whose insides churn in the darkness. All of this surrounds us. When we sleep, they come out to make a life for themselves. They creep around us, like the gods of our dreams, and one day they will once again rule the world, because this world belongs to them.

By midday, Felisberto and Eloy have left. It's possible they won't return until tomorrow: two days ago they travelled into town with some half-rotten fruit and vegetables, and once they'd sold everything our land had yielded up to them, they got drunk. I could tell, because when they got back they gave off that same smell of fermentation you did when you died.

The sun burns the crown of my head as

I walk toward our house. Inside, only the women remain: the women and secrets. All houses must be filled with secrets that no one will ever decipher; just like ancient caves where death has been covered over by earth and rock, just like the river that carries blood downstream before allowing it to settle in its darkest regions, so must houses conceal so much death that they begin to weaken and crumble.

When Noah opens the door, I embrace her. She has bad, blotchy skin, like the women from town who consume only bread and sugary water. I have brought with me all I have: the Book, a box of herbs, and my insects. I pull the box along on the end of a string, as I used to when I was a child and would bring home grubs and caterpillars. They don't even see it; they can only see the past in me, when I was weak and inoffensive.

Noah calls out to Sarai and Mara, and all three embrace me. There's no need for me to say anything; they feel so sorry for me that Sarai leads me to the bathroom and fills the tub. I leave the box to one side and sink into the hot water which, after so long, feels strange to me. Sarai touches my swollen chest, covered in tiny spots like red moles. I take her hand and make her trace them like a constellation.

When I step out of the tub, Sarai dresses me in clean white clothes. And that sensation of linen on my skin is as uncomfortable as the first day outside the womb, as roots out of the ground. But it doesn't matter. We go downstairs to the kitchen together, where Mara is stirring a great steaming pot.

"Let me help," I say. And all three turn to look at me in distress, as though my voice were coming from somewhere dark and damp, somewhere that frightens them.

"Like before," I add.

I feel my broken voice, which is almost a whisper. I have to make an effort to speak. Mara takes my hands and helps me stir.

All four of us sit down at the table, and Noah makes us pray before eating. I close my eyes, but it isn't her god I'm praying to.

When we finish, hands still in prayer position, I look at Sarai.

"I accept what you told me. I want to go."

She stands, walks over to my chair, and

crouches down until her head rests on my chest. I part her hair in strands; her scalp is swollen with louse bites. Perhaps her insides look the same.

Sarai rises slowly and leaves the kitchen, her long, embroidered skirt and dark hair swaying from side to side. Only now do I notice that she is wearing woollen gloves, but it doesn't matter, we're suspended in the past. Mara and Noah move about the kitchen, preparing something for me to take on my journey, and I go over to my box of leaves and insects and sit down beside it.

I place the index finger of one hand across the thumb of the other, and then reverse this, over and over. Mamá used to say this was how you stitched time, father, and she taught me how to wait.

OUR DEAD SKIN

It was already morning when they brought my mother out of the house. Everything was covered in that murky film of water left by the hail. Eloy carried her like the deer they'd brought in on the first day they slept inside our house. Sarai had emerged from the barn dressed in her uniform and sat me on her lap, which was warm, because the uniform had just been ironed. "They're taking her to a place where she can get better, Lucas," she told me.

"Go and say goodbye, go on," she added.

She lowered me from her lap, holding me by the underarms. I began to walk, but became frightened and looked back; Sarai was staring at her chicken hand. When she noticed me looking, she hid it beneath the other one. She used to do that with strangers, but had always let me see it.

I went over to the carriage and, as Felisberto and Eloy saddled up the horses, sat beside my mother and combed her hair. Very fine strands stuck to my fingers. I tried to slip them into my pocket, but they flew away. My mother was sleeping, her cold, damp face resembling those of old crucifixes: at once luminous and agonized. "Get out of here," said Felisberto, and you, father, came running out, shielding yourself from the faint lingering drizzle with a newspaper. You handed Felisberto an envelope and grabbed hold of my hand as you spoke quietly to him. At the time, I was unable to hear the name of the town where the sanatorium could be found. And it would take me a long while to track it down, father.

At that moment I began to struggle, managing to break free from you and run over to mamá and kiss her brow. She clasped my right hand between her hands and her cheek, holding on tightly and whispering in my ear, leaving that soft breath inside me forever: "Leave here, Lucas, and don't come back."

I didn't release her hand, but she'd already let me go. It was Sarai who came to lead me away from the carriage, doing so only moments before Eloy yanked on the reins with such force that I had to step back to avoid being caught by the rear wheel. I didn't even cry. It was like a moment removed from time, my body yet to be touched by the pain of that departure, although it would be, later, over and over again. The horses and carriage vanished, and it would take them two days to return, without my mother this time.

All that morning you remained locked away in your study, father. Afraid.

Fear never keeps its big mouth shut. If a person is afraid, they should fill themselves up with it, but never allow it to be seen by others. It's a bit like going around carrying one's own severed head: it attracts attention. And you, father, went around carrying your head in your hand from that day forward.

In the afternoon, I saw you hobble out of your study. You returned after lunch with a cane to help you walk. No matter how often

Sarai, Noah, or Mara asked what had happened, you wouldn't say a thing. When Felisberto and Eloy returned, you began to avoid being seen by them. You would leave while they were out, and when you were at home you shut yourself in and forbade anyone from entering your study. You were leaving traces of your fear everywhere. You'd begun hiding inside your own home.

That night was the last time I spoke to you, father. Do you remember what you told me? You had me come into your study and sit across from you, but it was already too late.

"Lucas, what does God consider sacred?"

I loathed you, father. I looked at you and felt loathing. I'd imagined you dead many times during the night, my body covered in sweat; I imagined you no longer there, and only then was I able to sleep. That loathing mesmerized me. And, in that moment, I could not respond to you because my loathing had sealed off my voice, just as a cow's milk dries up when it is frightened, and the calf, hungry and thirsty in the dead of night, suckles and cries and wastes away.

"What does God consider sacred? It's a question!"

"I'm not sure," I responded, in a broken voice.

"Answer me, damn it!"

"I don't know."

"Do you want to know what God considers sacred? Everything that rots, Lucas. Plants, animals, man, shit."

"I don't understand you, father."

"Of course you don't. Get out of here."

I don't know if you've ever tried to describe the geography of a desperate face, father, but it resembles a volcanic island after the lava has cooled and formed uneven dips and ridges, all rugged and inhuman.

This was your face on that night, deformed by a reality you'd only now perceived. It was your sunken eyes filled with darkness that made me flee that place. As I backed out of the study like someone trying to avoid waking a corpse, I left you with your head in your hands. You were slouched over the desk, unable to look at me, with one leg crossed over the other as your right foot trembled underneath the table.

And then I noticed your diseased ankle. That's what I saw. Your ankle with its dead skin. Recent, yes. But dead. Just like Eloy's foot.

FELISBERTO

On carnival nights, God covers his eyes; the air fills with a ripe odor, underarms are permanently warm, women stop wearing petticoats, and in the walls and pathways of houses, between bricks, stones, and paving slabs, clumps of clover, lady's bedstraw, and white goosefoot sprout.

A carnival party was Felisberto's idea for celebrating the harvest, and you, father, like a frightened child, obeyed his every instruction. And so there was music from the town band, the saxophone played by a tiny man with muscular arms and scrawny legs; and there were long tables laden with pork—stewed and fried—as well as chicharrones that crumbled in the mouth. There was aguardiente, all the aguardiente from your cellar laid out on the table, and also wine.

Noah and Mara were decked out in jewelry and had changed out of their smock uniforms, and were in dresses they'd ordered from who knows where, looking like relics from another century: covered in lace and adornments, beads and muslin frills.

Sarai was wearing a dress too, but hers was a black velvet gown with fewer embellishments than those of the others, and her hair, also black, tumbled down her back. Her breasts, which had previously resembled the mounds of dirt where I collected earthworms, were now large and voluminous, with no gully between them.

And this is how they served the food, trapped within those dresses that seemed to move of their own accord. My nursemaids were carried along inside, their feet seeming to float above the ground. Imprisoned by muslin phantoms.

And there was music all night long, and all night long people drank what they wanted and more. I skulked around the house into the early hours, observing how the clamor took over everything. One could hear the rhythm of the pasodoble and the melodies of sad pasillos mixed with sweat. The men's faces were turning large and red, and their chests perspired beneath those linen waistcoats that seemed attached to their shirts; there was no other explanation for why they should continue wearing them. Noah's and Mara's faces were completely disfigured by alcohol, and they were being passed from arm to arm, grabbed by the waist, pulled this way and that, ventriloquist dolls with smiles like straight lines.

There was a deep sense of desolation that dissolved in the alcohol vapors, and a darkness that seeped into the twilight as the sun tried desperately to break through.

In the early hours of the morning, the rain began to pound heavily on the roof, causing a commotion like an army of children beating pots and pans. But it was merely a tantrum from the sky, for it soon eased, to be replaced by a tepid drizzle that accompanied the men as they staggered from the house.

Barely wet, they started singing:

Oh what a foolish carnival this life is!
Oh what sweet consolation, death!

They walked along the dirt track leading into town. Among them were the barkeepers, the plump lawyers that worked in their tiny offices while surrounded by yellowing papers, Doctor Ruilova, the Moratti brothers, and even Father Hetz and his entourage of seminarists who lagged behind, advancing single file with their black cassocks tearing through the wind like crows' feathers in the morning.

Once the house had emptied out, I went to my mother's garden. I did this every night, returning to the garden to feel safe.

By that time, the garden had already been destroyed, though there were still dandelions everywhere, obstinate and prepared to grow any place they could. That's where I found you, father, sitting on an old bench, your eyes closed and face distorted. I wanted to come closer, but Felisberto arrived, whistling as he walked, his misshapen body seeming to need to settle back into position after every step he took. "Come here," he yelled. And I went, walking through the drizzle, crossing my mother's garden and going over to where Felisberto stood, halting to the right of this man who was not my father.

You had your eyes closed, your eyelids were puffy and your skin was turning red; the corners of your lips had filled with dry white saliva. You wheezed and mumbled until you went still, your head falling to one side and a small amount of vomit beginning to dribble from your mouth. Then Felisberto smacked your face with his right hand, which was red and knotted. "Your father won't wake up," he said, and let out a sordid laugh, full of phlegm. In the distance, the drunken singing of the carnival-goers could still be heard. And I watched and listened, father, without doing a thing, because what could I do if you didn't want me to save you? You didn't want it! And it was not because of the loathing I had inside me, or because I didn't want to live with Napoleon, or because I'd imagined you dead, well and truly dead.

Felisberto brought over a bottle, pushed back your head, and poured in a stream of aguardiente. You regurgitated, and so much vomit came from your mouth that it seemed you must have drowned and were now being saved. That's what I imagined, that you would wake up. But you didn't.

"There's nothing we can do, we've tried everything," Felisberto protested theatrically to Eloy, before pressing his hands together, very earnestly, and saying: "Eternal rest grant unto him, O Lord."

Eloy spat out something he'd been chewing and Felisberto finished off the rest of the aguardiente in the bottle. And your body, father, damp and rigid, sitting on that bench, made me think of one of those dummies they burn in town on New Year's Eve, and I was quite certain that at some point we'd set fire to you and I would watch you reduce to ashes until you ceased to exist.

Until that moment, everything appeared to have been made of dreams, because dreams are more real than matter itself, so much so that they can be cruel and palpable, like teeth falling out or never-ending labyrinths. Dreams can encompass complete darkness; reality, on the other hand, is full of specks that make everything appear dirty. When your head, father, slid backwards with horrifying slowness, everything acquired the realistic quality of an inevitability. There it hung, your lips together, your closed eyes looking up to the sky, in a posture of supplication, to where your God would already be waiting for you.

Felisberto instructed Eloy and me to fetch shovels. It was Eloy who opened up the pit, father, I merely wrestled with the shovel. The men who'd poured out of our house had disappeared, yet the murmur of their song persisted: I heard them while my hands were covered in dirt.

Felisberto stood before me.

Seen from the ground, he appeared composed of a single great deformed bone from which protruded the lumps that somehow formed his face, arms, and hands; and especially his fingers, which were large and amorphous. "Come on, sink that shovel in," he told me. "One thrust, then you bring up the earth." That's what I did. I sank the shovel in as if it were a machete, and something broke. A stream of water began to bubble up. "Useless little shit," he spat.

We kept digging until morning, until that quagmire had become a deep, cold pit. Felisberto lifted your body, which already smelled rotten, the head still dangling, and carried it over to the hole.

When we began covering your body with earth, father, day was already breaking. The first thing I covered was your face. We continued to shovel in the earth. It was full of ants and roots, father, worms and spiders that wriggled and covered the few bits of your skin that were still visible.

By the time the day had filled with light, your pit was no longer deep, father, it was a compact black mass of mud and miniscule beings that were starting to inhabit your body.

Sometimes, when I cease to hear the hallowed sound of wings, I return to that final night of carnival, when God had his eyes shut tight as I shifted earth to cover your body, father, and the whole world trembled in my hands.

IMAGO

Sarai has her feet stretched out. She's rigid, and although her eyes are open, she isn't looking at me; she has been trembling and sweating for some time. I clasp her hand, the good hand, and she squeezes so tightly that my fingers turn numb. Noah and Mara closed their eyes hours ago, but every so often they are jolted by a spasm. Although they've already vomited up the contents of their stomachs, something invades their bodies, like lingering bursts of electricity. Yet I know they're no longer there.

This is all happening to them because they are cyclops in stagnant water, because none of my insects have accepted them into our kingdom. Before Sarai closes her eyes, my scorpions have almost reached her mouth, and my heart is in my throat. I remove them and trickle oleander water over her lips.

I caress her throat, my fingers moving up and down along her trachea. It isn't evil that moves me, father, but I must do this to prevent her suffering. "A little water and then sleep will come," I tell her. "Now stop breathing like that, be a good girl."

I returned to our house without knowing why, father, but now I love what I see. I finally understand everything: the sacred language of dead bodies, the fertility of the dark and the damp, natural grottos and the men who've imitated them to build their temples, the effervescence of life in waste and decay, the cosmos contained within a being the size of a pinhead.

Before nightfall, Sarai, Noah, and Mara have all stopped breathing and an immaculate silence is born inside this house. For the first time, I feel relief.

I hear the ticking of the pendulum clock; I should hurry. It's possible Elmur will arrive before they do, and, if that's the case, he'll have to stay with us forever. Nobody is leaving this house, father, and nobody will ever get inside again. Before striking the hour, the clock takes a breath. I feel vertigo on hearing the mechanism whir, like a dinosaur inhaling into its great stomach. And it doesn't pause. Time imposes itself with every chime.

I wander through each room and know they are there, that they always have been. That, inside this house, only they will remain, miniscule beings that will outlast us. Only flesh can save us.

I go to Felisberto and Eloy's room. I take the wooden box containing the old keys reeking of decay. In the last light of evening, I go outside to look for wood and, surrounded by the garden animals, bury the box crammed with keys like the bones of an old rotten corpse; I also bury the keys to our house, father. When I return, before locking the door from within, I gaze for the last time at the mountains, the ones my mother had been able to see for days from that room of death where you sent her. I watch them turn into their own shadows and know that tomorrow they will still be there, as will the path leading into town. I know too that thistles, ironwort, and poppies will invade all this land

and cover our adobe walls like a carpet, and that inside, father, will remain all of those beings that to you appeared insignificant.

Inside and outside this house, nothing will be left but the tenuous sound of climbing weeds and the subtle drone of the insects inhabiting them.

And that will be the miracle, father, a sacred and present miracle.

Now I'm the one standing on an old chair, closing all of the shutters and doors to this house. But this time I won't let them in. Even if they return, I won't open a single door to them. And without us on the inside, they will head far away from this old land, father.

Our skin will no longer serve as their cloak. They will have nowhere to take refuge; even if the house were to allow them back in, even if they slept beside my body, they would be like Sarai's headlice, who right now must be fleeing into exile from her cold dead corpse.

One on top of another, I nail the boards, window by window, door by door. There will be no more floods, invaders, visitors, men at midnight, no prayers, curses, or Father, Son, and Holy Spirit to rule over us.

Only a god with the power to dissolve within infinite matter would have been capable of eliminating all the evil in the world. That is what we ourselves will do, and over our house shall descend only clouds of flies, coming in search of what is left.

When I finish, father, I lie down next to Sarai, remove her woollen glove and clasp her decrepit hand, because I'm no longer afraid of her dead skin, nor the putrefaction that surrounds us. Because everything that rots is sacred, everything that rots is called life. Isn't that right, father?

The resurrection of our flesh is a miracle. There is no spirit that ascends, only a body that breaks down and descends in spirals through the earth, forming a more perfect and symmetrical existence.

Hallowed melody that whispers and transforms.

Señorita Nancy approaches; now it is she who watches me. She perches on my chest, and we are one. The oleander is slow to take effect on me, but the night's darkness has started calling to them.

Before I close my eyes, a frenetic sound takes over everything.

In the distance I hear a knock on the door, and my heart, which was fading, pounds loudly for a few moments. But the sound has begun to turn into an echo, as if coming from a dream, and inside my head everything fills with the sacred sound of fluttering wings.

Hallowed music, hallowed melody that whispers.

It's like listening to a thousand hands tearing at the walls, desperate to break free. Like listening to the consciousness of the earth itself. Like hearing thousands of frightened hearts beating around you, all viscera, all pulse.

And all else in the world goes silent.

I hear only the insects and a whistle that comes from within, a sharp whistle that sends me to sleep and turns everything damp, forcing me to relinquish my words and liquify my insides. It comes from this dying body and descends toward that which sings, which is the earth, which is cicadas, which are wings, which is my mother's voice,

a stream of water, like a whisper:
    "I'm the Queen of the Arthropods."
    But this isn't actually my mother's voice.
    No one remembers the voices of their dead.

VICTOR MEADOWCROFT is a translator from Spanish and Portuguese and a graduate of the University of East Anglia's MA in Literary Translation program. His translations of works by María Fernanda Ampuero, Itamar Vieira Junior, and Murilo Rublão have appeared in the literary journals *Latin American Literature Today* and *Mānoa: A Pacific Journal of International Writing*. His cotranslation with Anne McLean of *Stranger to the Moon* by prizewinning Colombian author Evelio Rosero was recently published.

On the Design

As book design is an integral part of the reading experience, we would like to acknowledge the work of those who shaped the form in which the story is housed.

Tessa van der Waals (Netherlands) is responsible for the cover design, cover typography, and art direction of all World Editions books. She works in the internationally renowned tradition of Dutch Design. Her bright and powerful visual aesthetic maintains a harmony between image and typography and captures the unique atmosphere of each book. She works closely with internationally celebrated photographers, artists, and letter designers. Her work has frequently been awarded prizes for Best Dutch Book Design.

The insects on the cover, and inside the novel, are drawn by internationally renowned Dutch illustrator Annemarie van Haeringen. Insects usually seem anonymous and are often irritating when we encounter them in real life, but Van Haeringen found herself drawing them with personalities: one might be wicked, the next a bit daft—rather like people. The fonts used are Draft Natural, designed by Ryan Martinson (Yellow Design Studio), and Harting Plain, from David Rakowski—both chosen because of their organic look, and the fading characters, expressing decay.

Suzan Beijer (Netherlands) is responsible for the typography and careful interior book design of all World Editions titles.

The text on the inside covers and the press quotes are set in Circular, designed by Laurenz Brunner (Switzerland) and published by Swiss type foundry Lineto.

All World Editions books are set in the typeface Dolly, specifically designed for book typography. Dolly creates a warm page image perfect for an enjoyable reading experience. This typeface is designed by Underware, a European collective formed by Bas Jacobs (Netherlands), Akiem Holmling (Germany), and Sami Kortemäki (Finland) Underware are also the creators of the World Editions logo, which meets the design requirement that "a strong shape can always be drawn with a toe in the sand."